TEMPTATION

Part 2

Affairs of the Heart Series ~ London

KEW TOWNSEND

Tremmelle Publishing

HOLLYWOOD, CALIFORNIA

© 2016 Tremmelle Publishing. United States
© 2015 Cover Design by Sparkle Graphics
© 2015 Cover images by Ruediger Rau; By-Studio
© 2015 Book Cover Layout by Jesse Kimmel-Freeman
© 2014 Interior Layout BookDesignTemplates.com

Sign up for NEWSLETTER at www.kewtownsend.com

TEMPTATION/KEW TOWNSEND
ISBN 978-06924988-9-7

Affairs of the Heart Series
London

HEART (Part 1)
TEMPTATION (Part 2)

Forthcoming

PROMISES (Part 3)
DEVOTED (Part 4)
BETRAYAL (Part 5)

Sign up for Newsletter

kewtownsend.com

CONTENTS

Chapter One

NOT THE ONLY ONE

1989

London, England

Day 2

olly Hill stood gazing into Kaine Walker's expectant Technicolor blue eyes, shaded by the longest, darkest, lashes she'd ever seen. Never had a man watched her with such wickedness. Everything inside her swelled, and thicken as his intense gaze eyes locked onto hers, and told her he'd meant every word he had been saying.

Breathless, Holly smoothly slid her hands up Kaine's strong forearms. The tips of her toes barely touched the floor and she didn't understand why her mind, body, and soul longed for him. She sighed after inhaling another long ragged breath and gasped for another. Undoubtedly, her eyes registered stunned.

And as if to drive the point home, Kaine repeated the lyrics in a lover's whisper, "Never leave me, now that I've found you."

His eyes told her he promised to make her feel like this forever.

I won't leave you, ever, she silently promised.

Had she heard those perfect words? Wasn't it true that when one went crazy, they didn't know it happened? Had her mind snapped, and lunacy had slipped in quietly? She didn't care as she closed her eyes, waiting for this dream weaver to vanish. However, this seemed to be no dream. Kaine appeared real. A flesh, and blood man, a magnificent man, so perfect in every way. His direct way of staring at her cut beyond any polite interest or genuine curiosity. Dryness swept her throat as her heartbeat quickened. He seemed perfectly content to hold her as his fullness relaxed against her. His gorgeous, blue eyes stared into hers, mysterious, and dark, smoldering with a hint of hopefulness.

It was then that she realized he was waiting for her answer. Here was another drop-dead gorgeous man enticing her to go with him. Now she understood why Luka had cautioned her about Kaine. How pampered, and spoiled he was, and always got what he wanted because Luka knew Kaine would want her.

Her breathing became harder to control.

Kaine Walker, rock star, wore none of the arrogance she would have expected. His eyes glowed with a new innocence. His breath smelled sweet, no taste of alcohol. His behavior seemed normal under the circumstances. He didn't seem as if he relied on drugs, no, his only crime, to be devastatingly beautiful.

Kaine's face had chiseled features that would have inspired

any master painter, his sculptured chest a masterpiece. His full lips, were heart-shaped, the kissable kind of lips that screamed kiss me breathless, again, and again, and again and never stop.

Moreover, there was something so familiar about his handsome face. His dark, brown hair hung long as if a romantic time traveler, lost, and alone in the twentieth century. His mysterious, blue eyes seemed confused by how he had landed here.

Like a sudden awakening, the room came alive all around her, gaining momentum, until scores of feet stomped. Hardy applause followed the howling and whistles echoing from the surrounding darkness. All the while, the mist continued to curl around her feet.

"Brilliant!" Raved Luka Hunter clapping vigorously. He cut through the smoky haze that gave the atmosphere, and every entity there, that subtle touch of surrealism, creating a private world where only she and Kaine existed. And she damn well refused to leave. But like all fairy tales, there came the moment of reckoning, and this one arrived bringing an abrupt stop. Where was the happily-ever-after ending?

Luka moved close. Too, close.

With the spell broken and the enchantment fading, Holly's carnal performance became embarrassing, rising quickly to burn her cheeks.

What the hell had come over her?

Luka approached Kaine, who still held her wickedly close. Luka slapped Kaine on the back though not a brotherly gesture glanced at Holly and praised with a congratulatory tone.

"Brilliant work." He glanced to Kaine and agreeably added. "You can let go of this beautiful woman. Lady's with me."

Holly saw the tension flash between them. What was it with those two?

Without missing a beat, Luka turned, and leaned next to her cheek, nuzzled her, and kissed her mouth quickly with the familiarity of a lover.

Holly thought to kiss him back as Kaine let go of her.

She passed into Luka's arms.

Luka kissed her again, taking his fill, and when sure he'd made his point, broke the kiss, and commended her.

"You put on a smashing performance. Thinking of me during that kiss?" He bragged, marking his territory, glancing back to Kaine. Luka wore an expression of puzzlement and asked. "I don't remember anything in the revised script about kissing her?"

"Never saw a script. I reacted as you directed me. Followed how I felt."

In stride, Luka continued, "That's not quite what I bloody meant. Still kissing women for sport, aren't you, Kaine?" The sarcasm thick and he nudged Kaine on his arm with his elbow, as a buddy would. However, these men seemed far from friends, judging by the insufferable looks passing between them.

Luka's stinging words crushed Holly but did not match the wounded look in his eyes. He'd tried to hide his feelings, but she'd seen how she'd upset him with her provocative kiss. Now, Luka set the record straight, protecting her from this womanizing rock star. Would she expect anything less from Luka? He cared for her, and she had displayed her raw emotions for Kaine, like a gutted fish, inviting the whole world into watch. In the meantime, to her horror, she had forgotten about Luka, the cameras, the Hard Rock, and the world.

Holly closed her eyes and tried to deny the impossible situation that formed around her. Unfortunately, in those seconds, all that seemed important, was to stop Kaine from walking away. With one swallow of courage, she glanced up to look into Kaine's eyes. Did she misread the want she saw in his eyes? The knowing you can't have what's right in front of you.

Apparently, Kaine didn't care about Luka's sarcastic remark, and ignoring him leaned into her hair and asked loud enough for Luka to hear. "Say you'll wait for me? Don't leave me."

Dumbfounded by Kaine's bold invitation, Holly looked deeply into his eyes, intense eyes that feared she would say no. She had to react fast. Here she stood between Luka and Kaine.

Make a wise decision. How?

She looked to Luka, who instructed a stagehand, unaware that Kaine moved in on her, then looked back to Kaine whose eyes said, to hell with Luka — come with me. With a mixture of her head and her heart, she answered in a weak, indecisive tone.

"Maybe?"

"I'll take that as a yes," Kaine confirmed. His face lit up with a full, endearing smile that curled at the side of his lips flashing scrumptious dimples.

This was an all too familiar scenario of falling head-over-heels in love-at-first-sight with strange men and was wonderfully alarming.

Englishmen...

Kaine stepped back, but he allowed his hand to slide down her arm like a silken cord until his hand reached hers. Out of Luka's sight, he wrapped his fingers around her with the lightness of holding a feather.

She became keenly aware of where she stood — half in Luka's arms and holding hands with Kaine. The more she reviewed her erotic performance with Kaine, the hotter the humiliation burned her cheeks.

She slipped out of Luka's arms and dropped Kaine's light grasp, deciding to head for the darkness to disappear. And as if that wasn't the last of her problems, there's how to face her angel eyed Luka. How to explain Kaine's all-consuming charm? Or that Kaine had invited her to wait for him. Holly hung her head because she wanted to wait for Kaine more than anything in the world, except hurt Luka.

Holly took a step closer to the edge of the darkness surrounding the set.

But, Luka caught her hand, stopped her, and in an apologetic tone. "Forgive me." He gathered her closer to him. "I should have warned you straightaway that miserable lout might try something to compromise you. He's used to women making fools of themselves. He expects it. But I believe I've captured the explosive chemistry between the two of you. I couldn't capture it better with a second take. It's the element of surprise that made it combustible."

Holly stared into Luka's sparkling eyes as someone called him away. So, he had caught their explosive chemistry. She hadn't fallen into lunacy, and they all witnessed the magic. Luka had put her on notice he wouldn't send her back into the volatile arms of Kaine Walker, superstar.

Thankfully, she returned to her senses. She looked over at Luka issuing instructions. How close she'd come to throwing away her one chance for genuine happiness with Luka. Kaine was everything he was supposed to be, a rich, unbelievably elegant man that had too much damn charm for his own good. She chided herself on how stupidly she had acted and sighed with relief that she would not have to endure another hot, lingering kiss with Kaine. There would be no turning back if she stepped into his enchanting arms again because Kaine was the proverbial playing with fire, a rock star, the forbidden fruit, the stuff of which dreams were made. No, she would stay with her beautiful angel Luka. She would get over Mr. Walker's exquisite kiss, his seductive words, and his enticing blue eyes.

Somehow.

Luka's harsh words spun in her mind.

Expects women to make fools of themselves.

Well, maybe once — never twice. She would make it up to Luka tonight when alone in the dark. Yes, she would make passionate love to him, and force herself to forget Kaine. The problem was, Kaine's alluring scent had saturated her dress, and the taste of him still lingered in her mouth, even though Luka had tried to wipe it away. Holly shook her head until her hair cascaded all about her waist, trying to erase Kaine's perfect, dimpled-cheeked face, burned into her memory. How could she forget the touch of his hands caressing her skin that still tingled? No, it wouldn't be easy to forget him, especially his easy smile, and the raw silkiness of his voice. Or the smooth way, every move of his body, seduced and seized her senses? And what about his incredibly dazzling and impaling blue eyes that seemed to question the soundness of letting her go?

Thankfully, a sudden dose of indignation stepped in to protect Holly's fragile emotions. She looked around to find a retreat to figure out what to do with her aching body that required all of Kaine. She wondered how she could take this hot torment for a closer unity with Kaine, into bed that night and sanctify them with Luka.

How had this happened?

She needed to sort her muddled thoughts as she reviewed all the signs. The helplessness being molded next to Kaine's inviting body, her nipples hard, and responsive, her panties wet. She stood cold, alone and humiliated. She fought her own body that begged her to ignore her pride, and all sensibilities that coaxed her to leave her darling Luka, and head straight for the dreamy Kaine.

No! She screamed in the secret place in her mind.

But her torment wouldn't end. His rich, alluring fragrance had saturated her entire body and she wondered how to remove Kaine's exotic scent, a hint of amber mixed with a touch of floral, from all over her? One thing, she could grab a beer and hopefully remove the sweetness of his kiss that lingered, both in her mouth and on her lips.

On the heels of that thought, Holly plummeted into shame because it seemed she'd become a woman willing to set aside her principles to have Kaine. Her ragged emotions turned on her, and instead of enjoying the euphoric feelings ignited by Luka or the overwhelming charm of Kaine, white-hot anger rumbled through her.

She was tired of men controlling her. And trembling, she briskly walked across the dimly lit set to pierce the inky blackness laced with the ominous mist curling about her feet. She reached out for the bar like a blind lady.

She needed a new plan.

Chapter Two

IF I FELL

Holly summoned the bartender as she reached the bar, "I need a beer, please." She couldn't decide which hurt more, her foolish heart or crushed pride. A few days ago, all that concerned her was how to say no to Brett's insistence that they set a date to be married. Today she'd been passed back and forth between Luka and Kaine, two beautiful and powerful men in the music business.

Maybe these conflicting feelings confused her because she was a long way from home and on her own for the first time in her life. Though she ran in a complicated world of criminal law, she'd had little personal experience when it came to worldly and sophisticated men romantically interested in her. There had been seven years ago, but he'd been an uncomplicated, young man. Since then, she'd had a dead heart. Wasn't she about to enter a loveless marriage with Brett to avoid being devastated again? She only knew one thing. She felt alive for the first time and was bursting with raw, sexual feelings for Kaine and no place to put them.

A cool hand lightly grabbed onto her wrist, instantly irritating her. She hesitated. She didn't want to turn and find Luka because she didn't have any rational words to explain how much she wanted Kaine. She loathed herself for being at a loss for the right words to defend her erratic and duplicitous behavior. She didn't want to explain to a wonderful and kind man, the overwhelming experience of Kaine's irresistible magnetism that had almost convinced her to hurt Luka.

She took a deep breath and prepared to turn to confess her sins to Luka, but something inside her snapped like a brittle twig and decided to drop the topic.

That had been a wise idea because instead of Luka, she stared into the incredibly dreamy eyes of Kaine.

Kaine Walker, the devil incarnate and sinfully exquisite. The expression he wore was one of a bad boy tempting her with his seductive blue eyes. His long, lustrous brown hair flowed about his face as he loosely grasped her hand, forcing gentle electric shocks up her arm.

Kaine stepped in closer, dressed like an ad for Asset, an exclusive couture clothing line. He wore a long-sleeved, deep purple, banded-collar silk dress shirt, a richly scented Italian black leather vest that was unbuttoned, and black cashmere tweed, cuffed trousers. That's all she had noticed before he spoke.

"I am sorry, Miss Hill, may I explain?" He tested, with a husky voice, his gentle eyes pleading for her to listen. Without waiting for her answer, Kaine slid his long, slender fingers between hers as if her lover and his powerful touch became another soothing elixir to calm her.

She held onto him as if a dear old friend she hadn't seen in years while he led her to a dark, private area at the end of the bar. A dim ray of a stray light cast them into a hideaway of sorts seemingly far from the bustling crew but more importantly, far from Luka.

Holly released his hand and found it difficult to scale the bar stool wearing the suffocating dress. He impressed her with his manners as he offered to help her. She leaned on his strong and muscular arm, the dreamy scent of him so soft and familiar.

He ordered two mineral waters as Holly remembered she'd left her beer at the other end of the bar.

Holly twisted on a stool to get comfortable. A single, thick strand of hair fell in front of her face. She flinched as Kaine swiftly came to its rescue, pulling it back and draping it over her ear.

"May I call you Holly?" he asked politely with only a hint of a British accent.

Holly moved her head forward once as if to say yes, wondering why he wished to explain anything to her. Why would he give a damn? But to be bathed in Kaine's commanding presence made it difficult to keep a clear train of thought. One second she pondered what he wanted with her, in the next distracted by his elegant beauty as if lost in a trance. She stifled a laugh, realizing she sat in a nest of beautiful Englishmen.

Kaine leaned in close to her while he idly twisted a paper napkin between his fingers. "Miss Hill ... Holly, when I arrived, Luka briefed me on my marks and told me we had a new model for the shoot, and instructed me to enjoy myself. I'm never happy about doing these shoots because they are usually tedious and boring ... until I saw you.

"I blew off the rehearsal, but I assumed Luka had coached you. But when I saw you standing all alone waiting for me, well, I guess you sensed my thoughts. I apologize for my indiscreet behavior. I've little defense except I couldn't stop myself. You're so beautiful in my arms. It felt like we were alone, lost in the darkness and mist and I reacted, naturally. Please understand that I had to kiss you. I would have moved heaven and earth to kiss you at that moment."

Kaine dropped his head a little. Long, silken strands of hair fell forward as if a waterfall. He dropped the twisted napkins, to snag the locks with his fingers, raked his hand through his thick sable hair, and pulled a long lock behind his ear.

She understood, all too well. Kaine's assessment of the moment was correct. The world had stopped. To her delight, she hadn't been wrong. He'd wanted to kiss her every bit as much as she'd wanted. Holly from Beverly Hills, Kaine the rock star — wanted her close, oh, so close.

Wasn't life full of surprises?

Kaine's admission sent another raging heat of embarrassment to flush Holly's face. Again, her emotions clashed, frightening her. Should she stay with him? Or run from him? She needed to behave herself and decided to pretend to be in the courtroom. She put on a calm face and hoped her words spilled out coherently and informed him. "It's all right Mr. Walker. This has been an overwhelming experience for me too. First, the concert last night ..."

Kaine interrupted, "Please, call me Kaine. And you saw the concert last night?" He seemed confused.

"Yes, backstage. I won the CMT contest." She admitted ill at ease, still embarrassed by her timely contest winning. "Of course, you don't know I saw the concert since we weren't introduced last night, how silly of me."

"No, don't think that it's well ... you're so different from last night. The band told me when I arrived today that Luka took the contest winner around to show her the set. Chins wagged about how you look similar to an old friend of the bands. But that girl last night ... you today ... you're so different. You're magical. Beautiful ... I mean you were last night ... the most beautiful woman I'd ever seen."

Kaine stumbled over his words, not something she would have expected from a sophisticated and confident man of the world.

"Please, allow me to start over again. You're always beautiful, perhaps more when you're in my arms, kissing me delirious with all your passion."

He'd gone too far and Holly stiffened. But he'd caused her to wondered, exactly what did he mean by the most beautiful woman he's ever seen?

His face filled with a tender smile he meant only for her. His charm caught her off guard, and she instantly forgot her question because Kaine's scrumptious dimples made her want to reach out and cup his breathtakingly beautiful face in her hands.

Though she remained extremely self-conscience of her every move, she had to ask, "Why are you smiling at me like that?"

His words surprised her.

Kaine dropped his head and peered up at her amidst his lashes with a hint of shyness. "I'd hoped to meet that woman in Luka's arms last night. When he lifted your face, you looked dreamlike with the light glowing on you. It changed something inside me. You looked so exquisite, so damned desirable. All, I wanted to do, was to finish his job ... to kiss you forever. Holly,

I meet so many and so few I want to meet. But when I saw you, I was sure you're different, I wanted you."

"What do you mean to kiss me forever? What are you talking about, Kaine?" She was more confused. She tried to place him in the menagerie backstage. Hadn't he been down the hall having his ... sucked? Oh, it was all too awful. How could this wonderful man have such a darker side to him?

His gentle laugh prompted her to smile, as she gazed at his alluring face.

"It appears I don't have the lasting impression the fan magazines write so generously about me. Please, let me try to explain. Before every concert, I find a quiet place to be alone. To meditate, think, pray, call it what you want. I need to center myself before I step out in front of thousands. Anyway, last night I'd settled behind a stack of amps that turned out to be where Luka took you."

Holly strained to remember, but last night seemed like eons ago, and so much had happened. Where had the charismatic singer been backstage? That had been part of the problem. She couldn't see him perform, let alone meet him. She pushed her eyebrows together.

"You've forgotten? It's funny what the mind chooses to forget. Anyhow, back to my tale. At first, I assumed Luka had scored another groupie. She'd get her knees dusty, and such. As I watched on naturally, I became fascinated. Luka was acting different, because of you. Who were you? I had to have a closer look. You're not the usual type of woman Luka wants."

Holly forced a tired smile. "Yes, too often lately I have had this information pointed out." She ignored the agitating stab to her pride and rearranged herself on the stool.

"Oh, but that is the highest praise. Please, trust me. Luka didn't seem interested in you performing any sex act as is commonly expected. Plus you didn't respond to him like the others. You didn't dress like the others either in something so skimpy they leave nothing to the imagination. Your whole look and demeanor are like one of a lady, and as I'd said, Luka's a troll."

The incident flooded back with the force of a hurricane's landfall.

"You? The man that worked for the band?"

"Your words My Lady, not mine. My words, 'if I kissed you, I wouldn't leave you alone.'"

"I'm so sorry, Kaine. I misunderstood your reason for being there." She quickly scoured her mind, surprised at how difficult it was to remember the words of that conversation. "I remember your kindness and comforting touch. At first, I was so angry that you didn't make your presence known and so embarrassed. Please, accept my apology."

Kaine released a full smile. He gracefully picked up one of her hands and put it in his. "Don't you think I should apologize?" he asked as he combed his hair with his free hand and replaced the same rebellious lock of chin-length hair behind his ear. "I couldn't leave that touching scene. I watched on in amazement at Luka's reactions to you. I haven't seen Luka that taken with a woman since …" And his voice dropped instantly.

"Carrin?"

"I see. He's told you?"

"It's a heartbreaking story," she announced with a twist of sadness.

"He told you?" Kaine responded, sounding surprised.

"From everyone's reaction to me, I must have a strong resemblance."

"Uncanny resemblance Luka says. I see it, but not as strongly as he does. She's Luka's first love."

She recalled the CD with the song One Love. Luka undoubtedly wrote it for Carrin. "So it would appear from his guarded behavior with me."

"That's what caught my attention. He's a chap I hadn't seen in years. A man I use to call my best mate. Last night I realized how much I'd missed him. He's … I'll say it. Human!"

Holly choked on her next word. "Human! Luka? He's as much flesh-and-blood human male as I can handle."

Oops, had she said too much?

"I see." Kaine responded with a sharp tone and raised his perfectly arched, dark eyebrows. "I admit that was my reaction too. Luka's, how shall I say this? Let's say Luka is extremely popular with women. He usually takes them in stride and makes sure they don't complicate his life. He lives alone, travels alone. I mean without steady female companionship."

So Luka had painted an accurate picture. He had been alone. She wasn't sure she wanted to gain any more information about Luka's personal habits from Kaine. She sought to change the course of the exchange as she looked at Kaine and pensively asked, "Could he say the same about you?"

Kaine straightened his back, holding his head tall and regal. He smiled as if a king directing his court, tipped his head, and confessed. "Guilty as charged, My Lady. We've often been accused of being two-of-a-kind. But I can assure you there are many differences between us. My one hope is you'll come to see these."

Holly sat at a loss for how to respond. Did she want to spend more time with her angel Luka to fulfill all her adventurous fantasies while basking in his lusty attention? Or with Kaine and explore an extraordinary future with this beautiful romantic traveler.

Kaine must have sensed her confusion because he pleaded. "Give me a fair chance. Tell me what I have been accused of so I may explain."

Holly wondered if she should mention his sexual proclivities. It was none of her business anyway. Still, she wanted to understand how he participated in such a thing. She spoke in a steady voice. "I was supposed to be introduced to you at the concert, one of my many obligations winning the CMT contest."

"Obligation I've become?" He seemed amused allowing a boisterous laugh to follow while flashing a generous smile and the whitest teeth.

Holly carefully threw back a piece of her hair, not wishing to pull her hand from his, and ignoring his comment explained.

"You were nowhere to be found. One horrible woman backstage said you …"

"Yes? Where?"

"Down the hall — and they'd all agreed you were with a line of women waiting their turn … on their knees …"

She couldn't bring herself to say the foul words. But she'd said enough, if he was that sort of man, better he knew she been apprised of his decadent practices.

Kaine leisurely straightened his back slightly moving his head as if he understood. He took her other hand and covered both of them. He looked up and responded in a tone of 'I'm sorry you don't like me.' "I see. You believe I am a hedonistic rock star that indulges his every whim?"

"Kaine, I didn't say that." She protested.

"You thought it. Why not? Everyone does. I'm spoiled rotten. They all say I'm terrible. And they are all wrong. No one knows me anymore. I've been out of the public eye for four long years, and I swear I've changed."

"Please, Kaine. You don't owe me an explanation. I barely know you."

"Oh, but you do, all too well, My Lady. Otherwise, you'd never been able to kiss me into a delirium with all your fiery passion."

Would the heat that lashed her cheeks from that remark ever cool.

As if Kaine didn't notice her blush, he cautioned. "Holly, please listen. I want to know you, but understand Luka's been with me since the creation of the band. Luka knows I go and find a place to be alone before concerts. I've been doing it my entire career. He is still spinning the same ridiculous, adolescent story about me he always has, about the depraved rock star off having his way with young girls. He needs to realize it's a new era, safe sex, and all. Holly, please believe me. You saw where I sat, backstage … with you in my quiet place, waiting for the show to start between the two of you."

Holly bent her head. He spoke the truth. She looked up and allowed a half smile. "You didn't see much of a show. Nothing special happened. He didn't even kiss me."

"That's precisely what caught my attention. Luka never kissed you."

She was starting to lose interest in continuing the chat

about Luka with Kaine. She raised her chin higher to gaze at the most beautiful face, perfect face with a smooth, high forehead, with a touch of widow's peak. Eyes so blue rimmed with a thick black line that stared back at her with such adoration and respect, she blushed again.

"How long have you known Luka?" he asked casually, his bright, intelligent eyes revealing he needed details of their history.

"We met yesterday."

"Yesterday. At the concert?" he countered as if taken aback by the short timeline.

"Well, no, I met him by accident earlier in Chelsea."

"Away from his world of music? How interesting? An accident you say. What happened?"

It would appear even Kaine tried to piece together the details of this mystery. She appreciated his astute and inquisitive mind. She liked that in a man. Even so, she'd never describe her last twenty-four hours with Luka. "Let's suppose we met, and I saw him again at the concert."

"I'd venture to guess from what you're not telling me, you didn't know you had met my Luka Hunter in Chelsea."

Her facial expression must have told Kaine, he was right. He ran his fingers deep into his long, luxurious, dark brown, hair again that hung a few hands length below his shoulders. He exposed sideburns that edged his upper jaw up to the bottom of his ear lobe. He arched an eyebrow to warn her he was about to drop a bombshell.

"Have you slept with him?"

She swallowed to stop her head from spinning, she needed to end this conversation and get off the damned bar stool.

"What possible business is it of yours?"

Holly stared indignantly into Kaine's eyes. But she instantly softened. How truly exquisite he looked. His strong square jaw, his high cheekbones, his flawless face, no scars, only utter perfection. His skin was so pale in contrast to Luka's fresh suntanned face. His rose-colored lips wore a sheen left by his tongue when he'd run between his lips to wet them. Oh, those lips that were half-puckered and waiting for her, luring her in, as if, deliberately inviting her to kiss him again, and again, and again.

His forehead wrinkled intensifying Kaine's dark blue eyes that were haunting and patiently waiting for an answer. He was wondering if she slept with Luka. She glanced away and back at his questioning her. She saw he hoped it wasn't true and decided to stop letting him assume she'd made love with Luka.

Well, she hadn't.

"No," she revealed in a hushed tone, too embarrassed to tell him.

"That's what I mean, Holly. He's changed somehow. You've changed him. In the past, Luka would have stayed the night and moved on to the next woman who threw herself in his path."

She bit her bottom lip nervously.

"You've made your point. Can we drop this topic?" she asked, uncomfortable with the line of questioning.

Holly attempted to stand. Kaine had waded across a line she didn't want to encourage. She struggled to slide down the stool intending to put distance between them.

She shot Kaine a piercing look and spoke with a stiff bristle in her voice. "I can see this will get us nowhere. For the record since you, seem so interested in Luka's private life. You're right. I wasn't aware of who the hell he was. I didn't care then, and I don't care now. Shortly, we will be in Los Angeles, and I can forget all about Hurrikaine. If you're finished with this interview, I'll add this. I never threw myself in his path." She curtly added, "Or any other man's!" She included a sharp glance, staring straight into his amused eyes. Even if not entirely truthful, she'd never have this arrogant rock star thinking so.

Holly slipped her hand from under his and tried to squirm off the stool.

"Damn this dress!"

Kaine reached out to take hold of her elbow and stared straight into her eyes. Only she didn't find arrogant eyes, she saw she had hurt him, and his answer surprised her.

"I'm sorry." He offered. "You're correct. Your affair with Luka is none of my business. I never meant to upset you. On the contrary …"

"Affair?"

She blurted out, as she sat down and glanced into his eyes that said they're sorry he had pushed her away. She saw the questions building in his eyes, hoping she would tell him no — she would not continue her affair with Luka. But she couldn't, and her quiet response condemned her.

"Your silence says I'm correct. I won't ask again, My Lady."

She smiled, yet her heart wasn't in the pretense. She wondered if this was the attraction. Finally, she was someone Kaine couldn't have.

She spoke with a nervous laugh.

"You are two of a kind."

"Ahh ... we're not. There are many vital differences. I still hope you'll allow me to show you mine." He pointed out, trailing off as his mysterious eyes closed, looking as if preparing to kiss her again.

All she saw were the crescent shapes of his long dark eyelashes.

"No Kaine, I can't."

Kaine Walker finally heard the word no.

Chapter Three

SOMETHING TO TALK ABOUT

Wow! What the hell was Holly supposed to do? Where was the manual with clever one-liners when the world's most handsome man opened his eyes and melted her to the core of her existence with just a simple look?

Everyone that saw her arrive with Luka would expect her to leave with him. She looked across the room and caught a glimpse of sweet Luka issuing orders, doing his duty, her white knight, so equally stunning. Sitting next to her, with frustration lacing his blue eyes, was the mysterious dark knight. How in the hell had this happened?

She couldn't think about the fast moving situation any longer. It was like a train running out of control and she didn't dare jump off while in motion.

Mercifully, Lilly, the wardrobe woman, called out her name.

She took a quick swig of her mineral water and turned to

gaze helplessly into Kaine's disappointed eyes.

There was no need to say anymore — no covered it.

Holly moved to signal she would stand. She unhooked her heels from the lower rung of the stool. Kaine stood up to move toward her, close, oh, so close and offered to take the weight of her body against him.

She accepted his non-verbal assistance.

He wrapped his arms tightly around her waist, and lingered, holding her next to him. As a final plea, he laid his warm, smooth cheek against hers and buried his head in her shoulder. Kaine's warm, soft lips branded the sensitive skin of her neck as he let her slide ever so deliberately down the front of his body. His moist lips created a trail of sweet kisses to her ear.

Her arms went up naturally to coil about his neck, and between the maddening sensations coursing inside her body, she asked herself the provocative question.

Could a woman fall in love with two men at the same time?

What she didn't listen to was the silent answer from the quiet spot in the back of her mind.

YES!

With her conscious mind blocking the reply, no other answers arrive. The invisible sparks flying from him blinded her and overrode her good sense, realizing she never wanted to leave Kaine's devoted embrace.

While Kaine's strong arms squeezed her body tightly, his lips pressed against her ear saying, "I have one last shot. Shouldn't take me too long? Please, wait for me." His lips pressed her ear more insistently as if to convince her.

Holly slid down the front of his body until her toes barely touched the floor. She had to tell him. They would be difficult words to speak. And unable to disguise the distress in her voice she explained. "I can't Kaine. Luka expects me." Holly glanced away from his eyes that were tempting her, hoping to convince her to do otherwise.

Out of the mist, Luka walked up to them and chided. "Pair of you rehearsing for another take?"

Holly released Kaine instantly, stepped back, and sheepishly looked up to Luka to find him staring at her with a bitter edge in his eyes. A crisp chill passed through Holly. The only question was, how long did she have until she needed to choose between them?

She needed to get away from both dynamic men to think clearly.

Holly stood between her beautiful bookend men — Luka and Kaine — both so terribly handsome, tall, with electrifying blue eyes and such kissable lips. And yet, they were different in so many ways. There were different hair coloring and facial shape, but Kaine had the darling dimples. Their personalities were different too. Kaine seemed more sensual, and Luka more commanding. Kaine was right. There were differences between them, but this was not the time to begin counting them.

She wasn't sure what would happen next between the three of them as Kaine, and Luka eyed each other with contempt. Never in a million years would she have guessed these two handsome men would fight to spend time with her.

Fortunately, she did not have to stay there and see who was left standing when the dust settled. Lilly enthusiastically called for her again coming to her rescue. "Luka, Kaine, I need Holly, NOW."

Luka tore his intense glare from Kaine. "Go ahead, Babe,"

he said agreeably as his head swung back to Kaine as if a screen door. "Kaine, ready for the last shot?"

"Anytime you are Luka. Anytime."

Holly wasn't sure they were talking about the video shoot.

Kaine's tone of voice was condescending, intending to irritate Luka.

Instead of responding, Luka took Holly's hand and pulled her to him. His subtle response to mark his territory almost made Holly laugh. Only this was no laughing matter. Luka was dead serious.

Luka gently placed his warm cheek on hers and quietly directed into her ear. "Go with Lil."

He pulled away, turned to Lilly, and instructed. "When you are finished, show her where the caterer's tables are, and make her as comfortable as possible. She has a long wait ahead of her."

Holly trailed Lilly in silence, but as she rounded a corner, her curiosity got the best of her, and she snuck a peek back at the dynamic duo. To her amazement, she found Luka and Kaine laughing and carrying on as if fraternity brothers. What the hell was going on between them?

Holly turned and walked right into Lilly, who had patiently stopped to wait for her.

"Oh, that. Their relationship is one for the psychologists to figure out. I think classic love/hate."

Holly shook her head to clear her thoughts. She wished she knew them better to sort out what to think. But she sensed Lilly coming closer. She turned and smiled at her.

"Take my advice. Tread carefully Holly. I wouldn't want to be the woman that broke up their friendship. Whichever one of them wins the fair maiden would never be happy in exile from his best mate. He would end up hating the fair maiden. It's hard, each of them so unique, and smashingly gorgeous. But I wouldn't want to be placed in the unenviable position of having to choose between them."

Holly listened to the alarm go off in her head flashing, Warning! Warning! You're about to make a colossal mistake. Proceed with extreme caution.

Forty-five minutes later, Lilly led a freshly scrubbed Holly with day makeup, straight hair, and dressed in her street clothes, over to the catering table. Holly finished the last of a scrumptious curried chicken leg.

It was the fifth take, and it seemed everyone hoped it would be the last. The expanding crowd of ardent Hurrikaine fans threatened to burst beyond the heavily secured barriers to swallow up Kaine. Luka was visibly worried pressing his eyebrows together as he paced. Security was on Luka's back every second. There would be mutiny if Kaine were to take much longer on the set barely out of reach from his hundreds of loyal fans.

Holly stood behind camera one, wondering why Luka was pushing his luck with the rambunctious crowd. As she watched Kaine, she was impressed. She'd never seen any man command all the attention of his audience as he did. Everyone paled next to Kaine. Between shots, she observed his constant patience and continued kindness, signing autographs, standing endlessly with fans for photos, and allowing a large assortment of women to kiss him all over his face. She recalled Luka's abrasive comment, still kissing women for sport. She was finding out fast that when Kaine arrived, everybody's attention focused on him.

As the sun set behind Kaine, Luka was becoming more visibly agitated. He was off in a corner hollering at a lone cameraman. The stress of entertaining the massive crowd was evident on Kaine's face too. Who said life as a rock star was always fun?

Holly watched Kaine force one smile after another for his fans until she noticed a softness cross his face. He pulled his sunglasses down to the edge of his nose, and she saw a twinkle in his incredible blue eyes when he pinned her. He stared straight into hers and winked. A quick heat rushed to her face. She blushed again.

Luka bumped her shoulder to signal he'd witnessed Kaine flirting with her too. He counseled sharply, "At the risk of sounding like a bloody spoiled sport, I would recommend you stay as far away from Kaine Walker as you can. Forget him!"

Stunned by his harsh recommendation, she blurted.

"Why would you say that?"

"I see your interest — I also see his."

What a curious observation.

"Luka, please, I don't have any deep interest. True the kiss was surprising, but it's behind me, and he is sad."

"Sad?"

"Yes. Obviously, he has no one to love him, care for him."

"He has an enormous entourage willing to take care of his every whim and need." Luka maintained, with no concern.

"Oh, they are the hired help. He has no one who truly loves him." Holly sympathetically added, "He's like you and me." She looked into Luka's eyes to reinforce her words.

Luka wouldn't bend. "Don't waste your sympathy on him.

He's rich, selfish and catered to 'round the clock.'"

"He can't buy love, Luka. It's a rare and precious gift." Holly lingered a moment and grew quiet while looking at Luka. He stood before her with a perplexed look on his beautiful angel face.

"You aren't making out much better Luka. You are running and hiding from love ... no one to go home to ... travel with you."

"Who told you that?"

"Kaine, in so many words."

Luka's face softened, and yet he didn't want to give in an inch. He reached down, clasped her hand, and pulled her over behind stacks of equipment giving them a bit of privacy. He moved in close, oh, so close. His clean, fresh scent reminded her of the morning lying in his sensuous embrace. Those were wonderful moments with him because it had been so long since she'd belonged somewhere, to someone.

She knew how lonely these two men were. Their money hadn't brought them happiness. Luka words broke into her evaluation.

"You're bloody right about me, Babe."

He volunteered before his sweet lips kissed her from her cheek to her lips. There he covered her mouth and gently kissed her until her knees weakened forcing her to cling to him.

After satisfying himself, he pulled away and confided.

"You make me believe in love."

Holly hesitated, was he kidding her?

But something in his eyes said he wasn't. She pressed against him, laid her finger upon his lips, and confessed.

"I'm not what you think. I've been like you, empty for

what seems like forever. I'm not sure how much love I have to give anyone, especially you, or if it would ever be enough to make you forget."

She felt it was wise not to mention Carrin's name since she didn't have all the details of her mysterious departure.

"I'll take all you have."

"What if it's not enough?"

"Whatever you have, will be sufficient."

"You're so easy to please, Angel Eyes."

Luka threw back his head, heartily laughed, and pointed out.

"I forget you haven't known me that long. Anyone, you ask, would bloody well tell you differently. But here, today, perhaps there is a chance for you, and me, only...."

She watched Luka and turned to look at what had caught his attention.

It was Kaine.

"Stay away from …"

Luka allowed his beautiful blue eyes-to-die-for to complete the sentence, followed by his lips, brushing lightly against hers.

The moment was intense, explosive. Overcome, Holly surrendered once again to his powerful and provocative embrace. She moved to speak in a low tone in his ear.

"Luka, Luka, my sweet golden-haired angel, don't worry about Kaine."

At that moment, an interruption arrived, no, not his phone, but harsh, demanding words.

"LUKA! Get the fuck over here!"

It was Kaine's voice, loud, and authoritative, and he'd frightened her with his powerful command.

Luka ignored Kaine's directive letting it roll off him like water on a duck. He kissed her again quickly and pleaded.

"Listen to me. Don't let Kaine fool you. Don't become another of his many conquests. You've heard the rock music stories ... fucked, sucked, and abandoned.

Chapter Four

DESTINY

Luka's words were brutal and biting, unlike the Luka, she cared for, but he'd made his point. Luka had self-appointed himself as her protector, and she placed her hand on his arm.

"You can't go on protecting me. No matter what happens between you and me, or Kaine and me. You need to believe I can take care of myself."

He shook his head. Luka wasn't buying any of her speech. He was shaking his head as he turned muttering, "Not you too. That's what they all think of first, so many bloody fools taken in by Kaine's fake charm. He is not the typical, spoiled rock star. Watch how easily he works the crowd, always the professional. But I know the real Kaine. His first and only love is music, and he'll never marry." And he threw her a glance to go with caution.

Holly hoped she wasn't thinking too naïve, again. Luka pulled the megaphone to his lips, wet lips, she had kissed as if she would care for him all of her life.

He made an announcement to the crew. "That's the last

take. It will bloody well rain straightaway, and it's been a long fucking day."

Luka spoke with a civil tone to Kaine as he walked over to him. "Kaine, CMT will be pleased with the last take. Brilliant, really." His upbeat tone sounded forced as he extended his arm in a half-hearted manly hug, as a strained attempt to conceal his real feelings.

Always a gentleman, she thought.

Holly restrained the urge to run to Luka as he turned to her. His facial features were tense and grimaced. She wanted to stroke his face until he smiled at her, kissed her, held her close, and made her forget Kaine Walker, who stood directly behind him defiantly staring at her. And she wanted to ignore the burn of shame growing in her chest because if Luka looked at her, all he would find in her eyes was a betrayal. She'd never be able to conceal her thoughts about Kaine from Luka's sparkling blue eyes.

Holly was at war with herself. She wanted both of them. How would she decide if ever given the choice?

She rushed to Luka and hid her face on his broad shoulder, desperately hoping for an answer to arrive.

But it didn't.

However, other thoughts did. She wondered if Luka might have painted a bitter picture of Kaine, trying to discourage her, wanting to plant the subtle idea with his cryptic prophecy — he'll never marry. That was when she realized Luka was leaps and bound ahead of her thoughts. And she had to wonder why.

Holly moved behind Luka as he started issuing orders again. She admired the varied colors of gold spun into his flowing locks. His tight Levi's compelled her to run her hand from the inside of his thigh up over the seat of his pants then she wrapped herself around the back of him and held on for a long while. He didn't move but covered her hand resting over his heart with his, while he barked a few orders.

She rested her cheek against his back trying to analysis how much of these feelings were love. How much in love with Luka was she?

A quarter?

A half?

Half-in-love-with-Luka?

She seemed to have one name on her lips, the other man in her heart — but which was real?

Apparently, Kaine hadn't given up on her either, as he boldly walked up to her. He stood within inches of Luka and softly and politely invited her. "Luka's unavailable for another four or five hours. I was hoping for his permission, and, of course, yours that you would allow me to show you London's sights and culture, and take you to dinner?" Kaine threw a friendly, courteous look to Luka.

Luka turned in her arms breaking her embrace forcing Holly to step back and he charged within an inch of Kaine's face to lambast him. "You want me to say no? Don't take her, and act like a tosser? Bloody hell Kaine, you can show Holly any of the sights you fucking well please, that is with the lady's permission."

What an awful situation for everyone involved. Why hadn't she prepared faster? She'd had a premonition this would come. She thought fast. It would be boring, and tiresome waiting for Luka. There were only precious hours to see London. And to see them on Kaine's arm would be amazing. She suddenly pictured Scarlet O'Hara at the party trying to pick a beau for dinner. She shifted her glance from Luka to Kaine. Then from Kaine to Luka, who were awaiting her decision. It was an unbelievable moment!

With a soft voice, trying not to show too much excitement, and upset Luka, or encourage Kaine, she asked, "What did you have in mind, Kaine?"

"Places you haven't thought of, My Lady," Kaine enticed with words packed full of special meanings as he lifted an eyebrow and winked at her.

She scarcely restrained her shocked response, and she saw Kaine had met his goal to piss off Luka. Should she leave Luka? She looked at her beautiful Luka with his bloodshot eyes, his hollow cheeks, his parched lips. What he needed was a good night's rest, not spending it trying to entertain her. She wanted to reach out and touch his face that sported a shadow of dark whiskers.

He spoke as the gentleman he was, and he couldn't have astounded her more. "Go, Babe. Kaine's right, I'm here, or at the studio all night. Go with him. I'll ring you at the hotel if I get finished at a reasonable hour."

And so that's how it came to be that Luka encouraged her to go, pushing her toward Kaine. Was it his trust in her that motivated him? She looked at Kaine, his face glowing from the twist of fate.

She looked at Luka, who was bending close to her to kiss her meaningfully on the cheek. Apparently, it was all set. Holly didn't understand why after all Luka's warnings about Kaine, he was encouraging her to go with him? Was this a horrible test to see what her reaction would be?

Kaine instructed Luka, as almost an order. "See to it the lady has a place to wait for me."

Luka's face burned red-hot. His eyes were fuming, and it was then Holly finally understood. Luka may be the prestigious CMT representative, but he still worked for Kaine. Perhaps that explained the cutting edge that ran between the highly dominant males. Luka had no other choice but to hand her over to Kaine. Possibly, there wasn't an alternative, as Kaine had made it appear. She wondered how miserable Kaine would make Luka's life if he went against his wishes. Of course, there was the paranoiac thought, was this all a power play, executed by Kaine, and she was the pawn to put Luka in his place? She had so many thoughts, and none was comforting.

Luka threw Kaine a nasty look and cursed under his breath obviously irritated at Kaine's ordering him about. Holly felt another prick of guilt, as she accepted a nearby stool, Luka found for her to perch upon while Kaine hurried off to have his makeup removed. In the interim, the crew, and the band were quickly reduced to pranks and teasing. Everyone was tired, irritable, and ready to call it a day.

Her unrest stemmed from her recurring thoughts about drifting into the night with the worldly and sophisticated Kaine. What did she have to talk about other than her criminal cases at the firm? She might amuse him with anecdotes from her perspective as part of the defense team for the Collins' murder trial. There had been so many twists and turns that led to Mason Collins, verdict — not guilty — and surprised everyone, except Brett. She believed he'd murdered his filthy-rich, old, stupid wife, the weasel. Although they'd fought an uphill battle for the verdict, he was the last subject she wanted to talk about with

Kaine. What was left? Her mediocre life? A life that truly started two days ago when she'd left, Los Angeles.

"Holly."

A smooth voice called to her, the voice with no edges.

"Yes?" She replied, looking up to Kaine trying her best to control her obvious attraction to him.

"Let's catch a cab, have fun. Let me show you London." Kaine dared to suggest.

Did anyone say no? She had once and look how that turned out. Holly glanced around to say goodbye to Luka, but he'd vanished into the melee of confusion as the crew packed up the equipment. Weary, she spoke above a whisper, sounding as if she gave up, "I'm ready."

"You will see Luka again. I'm not kidnapping you." His tone playful, yet laced with a scrap of jealousy.

She decided it was good for Kaine to be on the defensive. "Let's go," she encouraged, smiling with a curl of caution about her lips.

Kaine walked closer, ensnaring her in his wondrous scent. He reached down, grasped her hand, and locked her fingers with his.

She boldly stared up into his eyes, searching. She still wondered if it was wise to leave with him.

But he squeezed her hand and said, "Last chance to run from me."

"Never." She declared with conviction. She wasn't afraid of Kaine Walker. Maybe that was the problem, she should be.

Kaine slipped out the rear door of the large building to hide from the enthusiastic crowd. He hailed a Hackney cab and directed a stunned cabby, who apparently recognized the pride of England.

"Parliament."

Holly sat back in the cab.

Close.

Too, close to Kaine. Overwhelmed by his presence, she was set on notice her surrender was imminent. His handsome appearance drew her nearer to him. He wore dark-blue 501 Levi's and a form-fit, purple tour T-shirt that read, Lost Dreams … Lost Illusions, and a Hurrikaine letterman jacket, with purple leather sleeves and black wool panels. A small Hurrikaine logo and his name 'Kaine' was stitched over his heart with gold thread.

If it had been after the sunset, Holly swore she would have been able to see the sparks flying from her body. She attempted to deny her fiery attraction to Kaine, and that made it exceedingly difficult to carry on any conversation. How was she going to make it to the end of the afternoon and especially into the night with this incredibly attractive and sexy man? So she tried to distract herself by looking out the cab window to devise a new plan.

Instead, Luka came to mind. Damn! Stuck working all night. Mmmm, Luka, how he brought a smile to her face. Her gentle angel, well, in retrospect, he wasn't that gentle. He seemed to be ferocious when pushed. All the same, he was her handsome golden angel, and how dear he was to her.

"I hope someday the thought of me will bring a smile to your face as you have now," Kaine spoke above a whisper, destroying the image of Luka.

"What makes you think it's not for you?"

"You haven't looked at me once since we got in this cab. I

would put my money on, Luka. He has a strong influence on you."

She turned to Kaine, and she should have warned herself about how devastatingly beautiful he would be inches from her. "Right again. I was thinking about Luka."

"I see Luka in your eyes. What's more, I see you in his. I'm so sorry I met you after him. Then perhaps that special look I see in your eyes would be for me."

Chapter Five

SOMETHING

The silence in the cab was deafening. Where was the comfort zone they'd shared at the Hard Rock Café? Her head was crowded with doubts, dreams, and desires. Yes, there lingered an intense ache to feel Kaine's warm lips on hers again.

Holly thought about how she would have never predicted that within a short span of two days, she would meet not one dynamic, and powerful man, but two. Or, that both would vie to lay claim to her. Luka's interest had rapidly increased from the second he'd touched her. Still, he had an agenda because she understood she held a strong resemblance to his first love Carrin.

Then there was Kaine. She couldn't quite piece together, how he had slipped into her life so smoothly out of the mist. Exactly what was his agenda? Was she part of a long recognized competition these men had shared for decades? Was the attraction to her to turn her attentions away from Luka, and then what? She realized she had to slow down and sort out her own agendas and the growing stockroom of new feelings.

She summoned her courage and decided to find equal ground and talk with Kaine. To forge a beginning, and hopefully, it would guide her to well-deserved answers, and at the least, back into his arms. She twisted to face Kaine. The moment jarred her, as he seemed absorbed with her, smiling at her, watching her.

She recoiled at once.

He leaned forward, with his free hand snagged another wild wisp of her copper hair hanging defiantly in her face, and draped it behind her ear. His hand continued around to the base of her neck.

Unable to stop her body from quivering, he pulled her half an inch from his face that she already adored. She tried to relax. Between inhaling Kaine's masculine scent and his warmth radiating all over her, Holly was losing her balance and was pleasantly dizzy. Kaine Walker was tempting her with his dreamy eyes, and all, she could do to save herself, was to close hers.

She heard her voice saying, "Kaine, I can't." Her words rode a shallow breath certain she'd lose control herself if his sweet, moist lips pressed hers. As it was, she quivered under his gentle touch. Still, he moved closer to her, his lips so close, his breath warm, and he moved closer until his smooth, soft lips lightly brushed hers, begging her to let him kiss her. She welcomed his masculine scent that commanded her full attention as his lips pressed harder on her.

Holly didn't want to fight him when his tongue outlined the seam of her lips, and with the last thought of Luka far behind her, she parted her lips and greeted Kaine's gentle kiss.

She was instantly lost in his enchanted spell. She responded quickly, brushing her tongue against his, matching the power of him, and her body flared with a growing heat. Her fingertips clasped the sides of his face, tracing his squared jaw line. She moved her body and pressed her breasts into him as he moved closer, slipping his hands around her waist, and up around her back, pulling her closer until her body crushed him. It wasn't long before her breaths quicken leaving her thoughts fragmented.

What the hell was she doing here? There they were again, the biting insecurities raising doubts about his sincerity. And she wasn't about to allow Kaine the satisfaction of knowing she was that willing, even if she was. She quickly tore away and gasped for air. Her face was hot, possibly flushed.

Kaine instantly apologized. "It's all right Holly. I have no right to insinuate myself on you ... you're Luka's lady." His tone was soft and filled with regret.

It was as if he had slapped her face. Luka's Lady! She had a title now. Luka's Lady. She caught another breath and conceded that, yes, but if she was Luka's Lady, then this behavior was appalling at best. To have Kaine add his understanding didn't make Holly feel more vindicated, but mostly traitorous.

However, she wasn't so sure she wanted to be Luka's lady anymore. Uneasy, she threw her luscious copper mane forward, pulling her long straight locks to hide her face. The scorch of self-consciousness burned as if she were a teenager. What must Kaine be thinking of her? First Luka, now him? What sort of unscrupulous woman was she? Would he be surprised to learn she wanted to make love to him here, this minute? Because she had to admit, he was unquestionably darling.

However, this duplicitous behavior wasn't any way for Luka's Lady to act. Luka's Lady. How had this happened? It hadn't been two days.

No, she wasn't Luka's lady. While she was on the subject, she would not become Brett's wife either!

The cab stopped with a jolt. Through the window, Holly admired the block-long sculptured, prickly-steeple monument to England's government system. Kaine signed an autograph, paid the cab driver and walked her beside the high gates protecting the great governing house of England.

Relieved to have something to concentrate on instead of Kaine, and Luka, Holly enjoyed herself, despite the fact that Kaine Walker was utterly intoxicating. For the next hour, Holly was in awe of the sights. Her favorite was the famous clock Big Ben, tall and bold, standing watch over London.

As his fans flocked to Kaine, he signed autographs and graciously posed for photos. Only once had he taken her hand to cross the street and had let go when they'd reached the other side. Every time she looked over Kaine was staring at her, and she wondered why. However, she did note that he'd been behaving like a gentleman toward her and kept a respectable distance.

She was almost grateful — almost.

Little-by-little it was growing colder, and a leather jacket no longer protected her from the brittle chill. The London sky had grown dark, thick with pregnant rain clouds in menacing shades of gray, and black that threatened to force all creatures large, and small to seek refuge from the promised storm. While Holly studied the dismal sky, she buttoned her thin jacket. She didn't notice Kaine moving closer to her.

"We'd better find shelter fast," he exclaimed, sweeping her up close to him by holding onto her elbow.

Being so near him put her in a dreamy mood and instantly whisked her away as if back in the fairy tale. Surely, any minute he would pick her up and set her on his white steed, and whisk her away to his castle, she the princess, and Kaine, the gallant prince. How silly the childish thoughts. But this was England, and she almost saw the cloud ship heading for Neverland.

They stopped in front of Buckingham Palace. Kaine moved behind her and wrapped his arms around her waist, like the first moments in the video. She was sure he would slide inside her skin when he gently turned her around in his arms and embraced her.

She looked up at him. There wasn't any way to escape the bluest eyes, she'd ever seen, growing full of expectation. But they made her afraid too because she saw he was as taken with her as she was with him. Then what would become of Luka?

Kaine spoke no words as he scooped her up pulling her closer into his arms, his lips did not test or ask to gain entrance.

She welcomed him, kissing him back, filling his mouth quickly, passionately as he kissed away the last of her opposition. She slipped her hands high inside his warm, cozy, band jacket as she lifted one of her legs to wrap around his, hopelessly lost in his wondrous passion.

It was then the skies sent a bolt of lightning into a black, waterlogged cloud, forcing it to burst open, and drench all caught below them. The refreshing drops of the rain forced Holly and Kaine to part, cooling their erupting passion. She laughed, and he joined her, as he rapidly covered his head with his jacket while protectively pulling her closer to him underneath the temporary shelter.

Holly stepped closer to Kaine — too close.

Kaine pointed to shelter, and she held on tightly to his waist as they hopped over and around reflecting rain puddles. Kaine's taunt muscles rippled under his skin, causing Holly to imagine holding his hips late at night. She shook her head. She had to stop considering the impossible dream of Kaine Walker, naked, making love to her because it was turning her insides out and would lead to so much trouble.

Holly and Kaine dashed around rain-blinded cars until they eventually arrived at a two-star hotel. They stood under the canopy, laughing at their drenched clothes. As the laughter subsided, they stood lost in each other.

His eyes said volumes, underscoring his emotions, inviting her to come closer if she would. He spoke with an edge in his tone and proposed. "I'm soaked. Will you go with me to my suite, dry off, and have dinner?"

"Well," she ventured already knowing her answer.

"Would it help My Lady, if I promised to be on my best behavior?"

Chapter Six

LET THERE BE LOVE

Kaine's rock star sanctuary in the Lainesbough Hotel was everything Holly expected, rich and tasteful. Holly spotted the heavy security stationed in the five-star hotel's lobby, and outside the private elevator that led to his penthouse. Surprisingly, the security made Holly feel more like a prisoner.

"Are you ever truly alone Kaine?"

"Only when I want it."

How often did that occur?

They stood dripping wet in the center of his suite. She was close, oh, so close to Kaine, and the moment was growing more, and more awkward. What the hell was she doing in Kaine Walker's suite?

Mercifully, he went to check his messages. The small water spot staining the thick carpet where she stood was spreading quickly. Her rain-drenched clothes clung to her shivering body, forcing her nipples to harden and protrude through the blood-red sweater. "I'm freezing." She insisted, fighting to stop her teeth from chattering.

A mischievous glint flashed in Kaine's dreamy eyes, but his long dark lashes made it hard for her to study his ulterior motives.

"I need to do something about these clothes," she warned.

"No trouble," he countered as if waking from a trance. "Tell me your size, and taste in clothes. I'll send my personal assistant out to buy you anything you want."

"That won't be necessary. Is there something I can put on until the hotel can dry, and press these garments?"

"If you're sure? Check out my closet. You'll find T-shirts, Levi's. There are belts and socks in the drawers." He offered, and politely excused himself by saying, "I need to wash out the gel Peter gobbed in my hair at the shoot straightaway. The rain has made it all one big bloody mess. There should be white terry cloth robes around somewhere. You're welcome to one until you find warm and comfortable clothes."

Holly moved her head as if in agreement with no alternative ideas for what to do.

Kaine called room service and disappeared into an adjoining room.

Holly twirled around and hugged herself. She was in London, in Kaine Walker's lavish hotel suite, with the toast of London, a few feet away. Holly listened to the shower start.

He's naked!

The potent images instantly popped into her mind. Soap bubbles leisurely beading and dripping down his dark chest hair.

She traced the path of soapsuds past his slim waist to his thin trail of hair leading her to erotic fantasies. Holly lingered dreaming of him, questioning if she'd make him howl with pleasure late in the dark, both lost in the fire of their love.

A flash of lightning pierced her extravagant dream of Kaine and returned to the task of finding something to wear. She surveyed his suite intrigued with his life on the road. It sounded so romantic traveling like a vagabond from city-to-city all over the world.

Strewn around the room were many books, perhaps as many as thirty or forty. His interests varied from the music industry magazines to hardback books about adventure and science fiction.

Holly laughed aloud. There wasn't much difference between the music industry magazines with the high-tech equipment musician's used these days and science fiction. On another table, was a tall pile of paperback westerns. She'd bet he'd be an outlaw at heart! She glanced down at the desk to a stack of messages, and mail. She browsed as her researcher's mind worked overtime compiling a preliminary profile of the mysterious singer. There were messages from magazines, newspapers, and TV, plus notes, and letters from internationally renowned names. Telegrams and faxes with messages of congratulation, invitations to anywhere, and everywhere, from kings to presidents. And another separate stack of invitations to sporting events and elite club grand openings.

Kaine Walker was in high demand judging by the fan letters, wedding proposals, and provocative sexual propositions. Growing more curious, Holly moved onto another small pile of personal requests. They asked for money to aid sick or dying children, families devastated by natural disasters, hospitals, and missionaries seeking his assistance. The next pile was special papers, as they were clipped and had a tiny Post-it note attached instructing — *Give them what they want, don't sign my name.*

Holly clasped her heart. Kaine, this wonderful man, turned out to be a champion of the people. She'd been correct about him not acting spoiled. He was a hero. Kaine cared about life, took responsibility to make a better world.

The last thick pile was marked "security." She thumbed through crank letters and threats. To her surprise, there were many death threats. She muttered to herself as her fairy tale dream world collapsed into a harsh, black reality. Kaine's world-class performance artistry had made him beloved by millions, but it also placed him in danger because of a few lunatics.

Holly sat in the desk chair, shivering, noticing how cold, and hungry she was as she examined the lavish suite. She saw leaning against the wall by the window, three of the finest guitars she had ever seen. There was a Fender 1957 Stratocaster, a customized, black, lacquered signature Stratocaster with 'Kaine' signed in gold script on the neck.

Her attention settled on the third guitar, an acoustic Martin and might even be the one he tuned backstage. She reverently picked it up to strum a few chords aware it was worth tens of thousands of dollars. The instrument's perfect melody lured her to play a few more chords as it resonated about in the lavish suite with the quality of sound only found in vintage, handmade wood.

On the table, were hastily written lyrics and scribbles, and she knew what they were. Words and fragments of songs committed to paper when the flash of creation had raced in Kaine's brilliant mind.

Perhaps one day she would listen to these meager snippets

in a number one song.

Yes, she remembered a long time ago, when many pieces of paper littered her purse.

Holly took a few minutes to play a few of half-written songs, following the chords on the scribbled notes. She felt his genius and understood why Kaine was the greatest singer/songwriter of his time. He understood his world well, he not only observed it, but apparently, he'd lived it.

Holly spotted a cassette/compact disk player with many audio tapes strewn everywhere. No question, the cassettes, were another way to protect his lyrics, and fragments of lines that circled his mind.

There were CDs of the blues guitarist John Roberts, along with a few newer artists, and bands never mentioned on L.A.'s FM radio stations. She leaned the guitar gently against the wall and popped in a Roberts CD and headed for Kaine's intimate world.

Holly peeked into Kaine's bedroom with the excitement of a maiden. She glanced around nervously. It was a sad sight. This room held no future for her. Surely, Luka would prevent her from curling up beside Kaine to make love.

No, this room was merely a sweet fantasy. She studied his massive queen-sized bed while she questioned if he truly slept alone. His muted-gold, bed cover shimmered like a magic carpet waiting to carry someone other than her to ecstasy. On the nightstand, were an assortment of throat sprays and lozenges. The rest of the bedroom was traditional European furnishings. It was clear the maid missed his suite or told not to disturb his privacy. His stage and casual designer clothes alike were strewn about and his Louis Vuitton luggage had opened wherever they'd landed.

Holly stepped over the clutter to enter an enormous walk-in closet. There was a long row of leather apparel hanging neatly in garment bags. Costumes, she assumed. The confined area reeked of his special scent — leather and cologne. She lingered inhaling his scent with a deep, purposeful breath until her head was reeling with memories of their kiss in the video. She reached out to touch an uncovered leather jacket and the sleeve was soft, supple, and smooth as his lips.

As if by magic, a melody floated from the shower. Kaine was humming, and then singing, "Now That I've Found You." She listened to the heartfelt, romantic lyrics. She smiled, thinking Luka failed to tell her that Kaine was also a loving, and caring man. From what Holly heard, this new song reflected a sensitive and tender man. A man whose lyrics said he had been alone too long.

There were no signs in the suite of another woman or legions of them, as she would have expected. There were no remnants of drugs, empty alcohol containers, or cigarettes. The entree, he'd ordered for dinner, was healthy, and light, with the finest champagne. He had the best the world offered, and she considered the possibility that Kaine would have her too.

Holly listened to Kaine's dreamy voice, a voice with no edges while picturing her hands unhurriedly gliding up and down his silky flesh. Caught up in the fantasy, Holly pulled off her wet jacket, soaked sweater, and a new bra, realizing too late, she'd left her other new purchases at the Hard Rock.

She left her heels by the door, pulled, and tugged off her wet slacks and panties then modeled for her reflection in the wardrobe mirror. She wasn't close to looking like the usual choice of stick-thin models for rock stars. At five-six and one hundred twenty-five pounds, sometimes she appeared slender — but never thin. She was happy with her full-sized breasts and all the running she'd squeezed in kept her muscles toned and firm.

Kaine, recaptured her thoughts once again, his breathy voice, his words of promise, tempting her, calling her to the edge of her sexual fantasies. She stood naked, hoping he would overlook his promise to be on his best behavior, and instead, overcome with lust, bury himself deep inside her, and lay, making sweet love, or hard and passionate love, until they no longer moved.

She cleared her head of the preposterous dreams. Yes, unfortunately, it was true. She had entertained all the same notions of Luka that morning.

"What the hell am I going to do?" She blurted out aloud to her reflection in the mirror.

She scanned the room for a terry cloth robe — nowhere in his things.

"Damn!" She figured out what she had to do. She leaned against the bathroom door and knocked lightly. She tapped harder and spoke aloud. "Kaine ... Kaine? I can't find the robe."

"Sorry, My Lady, they're in here, on the towel bar. Slip in and take one." He insisted, gurgling under the water.

Great! So unsure of herself, she grabbed a dry T-shirt from the floor and pulled it over her nude body, and freed her knotted, wet hair from the neckline of the shirt. She cautiously pushed open the door. Hot, lavender-scented steam assaulted her leaving her ill at ease so close to his nakedness. Luka certainly wouldn't understand her in Kaine's bathroom — especially with Kaine's fine, muscular body naked and in the shower, lathered in lavender bubbles.

The bath area was huge, glistening white, with gold scrolled trimmings, like an elegant spa. She searched for the towel rack, in the dense steam, and spotted the robe in question, w-a-y across the room, and too far for her to make the crossing.

She decided against the robe, but on her way out, she noticed a wide-toothed comb lying on the white marble counter. She needed to eliminate the tangles in her long wet hair. If it dried as is, to comb it later would be hell. She tiptoed over to the sink. Behind her, she listened to Kaine softly singing her favorite song from his latest CD, Moments of a Memory.

What a wonderful, and private interlude, listening to him confirm what real love was. She forgot where she was, and leaned against the sink, falling deeper into his crooning voice wondering why a man as kind and generous as Kaine lived and slept alone. A gorgeous man that could have any beautiful woman in the world he wanted. It was all there in his dreamy blue eyes, a man that had seen everything traveling the world. Intense eyes that testified he'd done anything and everything he'd wanted. Jaded eyes bored by it all. Lastly, dangerous eyes that could convince her, to join him and do things she'd never dreamed.

A strong sense of apprehension rushed and overcame her though it made no sense. She realized that perhaps Luka had found a cruel way to keep his promise to her when they'd been sitting at the bar at her hotel, and he'd vowed.

I'll do what I have to do. I promise you won't sleep alone.

Chapter Seven

HUNGRY

What a preposterous idea! She continued that train of thought and mumbled under her breath while standing in the damp mist of the palatial bathroom. A quick review of how her afternoon turned so radically was due to an incredible twist of fate, by attracting the rock stars' attention.

Holly pulled the comb through her uncooperative curly locks, inhaling short puffs of lavender scented mist. If nothing else happened to her in London, she'd always cherish these precious moments of peace, listening to Kaine's voice, sweetly seducing her lonely heart.

The longer Kaine sang the closer he drew Holly to the thin shroud that separated them. She imagined touching his soft lavender-scented skin.

To hell with thinking about him!

She boldly leaned over with all the bravery she could summon and peeked at him through a crack between the wall and the thin lining to admire his misty silhouette.

Kaine did not disappoint her. She was transfixed watching

the sinewy muscles in his shoulders rippling under his tight skin as his hands washed the lather from his long dark hair. Spellbound in awe, the simple act compelled her to watch him. His toned forearms and rounded biceps flexed as he washed the lather away. It took strength for her to refrain from reaching out to touch him and join in the ritual of rinsing the bubbles from his magnificent body.

Her gaze followed the smooth, shiny curves of his back down past the place where a tan line would have been. Down past his pale slim hips to his long, lean thighs. Even the bubbles clung to him, lingering, wanting to be near him. His calves were shapely like the joggers along L.A.'s beaches. And the light dusting of brown hair hugging his legs relaxed as the bubbles gave way. If she'd ever wanted one wish to come true, she wished he would turn around — now.

Request granted.

Kaine twisted his body under the shower nozzle to rinse the back of his hair. He stood in the steam, and it masked the top half of his body. All she saw was his flat stomach and rib cage shifting under his skin. Her hands trembled as she placed them behind her to prevent reaching out to touch him. Her gaze drifted down to where all her dreams could come true, but he lay relaxed, the darkness surrounding him as an enigma. His long, shape was thick and a beautiful flush color, resting on a bed of plump flesh. Delighted with what she saw, she dreamed of his true, aroused size.

From out of the mist, Kaine's face appeared. Before she could blush, he stood at the edge of the tub pulling back the curtain. "Do you like what you see?" He inquired in a good humor while his blue eyes dancing with mischief studied her.

His question stunned her, her reply more.

"You're magnificent!" She announced unable to stop herself.

He appeared unfettered as he smiled heartily and flashed his charming dimples. "I'm glad My Lady, approves," he said with a twist of shyness, tipped his head, her way, and laughed a comfortable laugh to put her at ease.

Holly stepped back. She turned to fade away.

Unexpectedly, Kaine caught her arm at the elbow.

"My Lady. Would you join me? Please?" He held out his right hand, palm up to her.

Before Holly could think of the correct words to answer, her body accepted his invitation while her eyes feasted on his naked, wet body. The stunning vision of him hypnotized her, his magnetism forced her to go to him. She had stepped into the mist with Kaine once upon a time and she remembered what happened.

The warm steam scenting the air was thick with his fragrant lavender shampoo. Overcome with an aggressive arousal, she wanted to taste his wet lips, to touch him everywhere, to eat him alive.

He moved closer to her.

She placed her hand on his chest and felt his pounding heart. He radiated pure, seductive magnetism. He moved with the grace of breathless masculinity until he pressed his lips to hers. Simultaneously, he reached down and lifted her soaked T-shirt.

She complied by raising her arms.

He broke their kiss momentarily as he pulled it over her head to complete the surrender.

This move signaled the beginning. She'd made her choice, and her last thought of Luka was for the hope that he would find it in his heart to forgive her.

She heard the wet T-shirt hit the floor outside the shower with a thud.

Kaine's lips pressed requiring her urgent attention. He awakened her with a trail of kisses. Then he drifted down her chin, to her neck as he moved to sit down on a ledge built into the wall of the shower and continued downward until he clasped onto her nipple. Kaine kissed her lightly then more fiercely.

It was impossible to concentrate as his silky-soft lips marked a blazing trail across her chest to the other nipple. His hands pushed her breasts together, and he sucked her sensitive nipples, first one, and then the other — his tongue hot, and insistent, licking, sucking, loving her. With each purposeful motion, her body rushed with flashing heat. She puffed out her chest pushing her nipple deeper into his mouth as she struggled to fortify herself with another ragged breath.

His hand drifted downward few inches to her stomach to rub her flesh lengthwise. His hand dropped nearer her dark, downy sanctuary. She anxiously awaited his touch, and when it arrived, the jolt burned like an electrical charge. The curling inferno that had started deep below her belly drew her closer to this mysterious man she already trusted with all her heart.

Unable to believe where she was, and not lost in any daydream, Holly glanced down to peek at Kaine's wet head nestled between her breasts. The water spray parted his long, dark hair. The magnificent Kaine Walker lavished her with his special affection for her, and the intimacy of him shattered any last doubts.

Moving closer to him, Holly savored his agile fingers as they stroked her skin exploring her caves and valleys. He focused his velvet lips on savoring each breast, encouraging his hot tongue to lick her chest, then upward to her neck where tiny bumps herald his arrival.

He hesitated.

Stood.

Kaine drew his hands up around her waist to pull her closer while he was sucking on her neck, following the line of her chin to her cheek where he moved deliberately toward her parted lips.

She closed her eyes, waiting as Kaine's warm, moist, tongue dipped in, almost shy. His restrained passion drove Holly to need him deeper. She closed her lips to hold him captive as her leg lifted and wrapped around his.

He pinned her body against the wall of the shower. One hand pulled her knee up higher and wrapped her leg around his waist while his other dropped to find his target and dipped his fingers in, then entered deeper.

Encouraged by his attention, her hands tenderly explored his strong shoulders, down each curve of his back, moving her hands lower, gradually, over his smooth cheeks. She pressed his hips into her, rubbing him, as he grew strong next to her feverish skin. She slipped her hand in-between them, inches from his powerful sex pressing her flesh, quickly growing in length. Holly tried to block out all thoughts. To take her time. She didn't want to maul Kaine's body as her thoughts dictated. She was in no hurry to leave paradise.

Lost in his overwhelming virility, conflicting thoughts fought her. She dreamed of dropping to her knees and tasting of him. Or should she guide him inside her? Instead, she placed her lips near his ear to whisper, "You feel so wonderful. You're not how I expected."

He pulled back to lay his forehead on the side of her head, and between sweet puffs of his breath into her ear asked, "How am I different from your expectations?"

She opened her glazed eyes while the blaze grew following his fingers that continued to explore the depths of her, bringing hot waves of pleasure to flash across her face. For a second, she remembered Luka's words — to let him watch the pleasure he brought as it crossed her face and she softly explained.

"You're strong, smooth, and so soft."

"Not all of me...." he countered.

So true, she smiled, awed by the final shape and size of Kaine. The possibilities for getting him to fit inside delighted her. She glanced up and drifting into his dreamy eyes as she placed her hand firmly around him. At first, he lurched as if her hand was scorching hot. But she took hold of him, gently, lovingly. Holly pulled, and stroked him up and down while her other hand traced the muscles of Kaine's back, and up each rib. Every inch of him she could reach gave her great pleasure. Holly allowed Kaine to watch her, closing her eyes again because the pleasure was becoming too immense as she drank in the warm rush of his love filling her lost and fractured heart. She never noticed how perfectly he mended together the fragmented pieces of her heart.

Long, sweet moments passed before Kaine pulled away from her and inquired. "You find me pleasing?"

The heat flushed her face again. And thankfully, the water spray covered her embarrassment. But she couldn't help herself from weakly acknowledging her confirmation as she opened her eyes to gaze at him.

"You're perfect ... it's been so ... since ... I ... touched a man like this. Well, maybe, never...."

"So long? Been a while since you've been with a man, maybe never? You include Luka in that scenario?" he asked with a twist of astonishment in the middle of the erotic scene unfolding.

"Luka and I were never this close." Well, they hadn't been. Luka wouldn't allow her to touch his body like this. This certainly wasn't the time to split hairs. So she explained. "It's been such a long time since I've made love. It shows?"

Kaine smiled wickedly as he studied her face, but quickly masked his thoughts from his eyes as if dismissing the mystery. Still the moment was magical as the water rained on him, kissing him as if a god.

He kissed her quickly spread his mouth apart with a smile, showing her his straight sexy teeth, and praised her judgment. "I'm glad you had the good sense to wait for the right man." He pointed out and chuckled. His bottom lip was wet with her kisses as his dreamy blue eyes teased her.

Holly was up for the bantering, yet her pride stiffened, even if Kaine's words melted her heart. She lifted an eyebrow and said to tease. "You think you are the right man for me?"

"I'm not sure if I am the right man for you. I know you my lovely lady — are the right woman for me."

"Why is that?"

He didn't hesitate. "I've never been kissed the way you kiss me. I've been kissed by ..."

Holly wouldn't let him finish. She challenged, "What

hundreds? Thousands? Are you an expert?"

Holly meant to joke with Kaine, to poke at his arrogance because of his reputation for kissing women as a sport. Instead, he misunderstood her remarks as jealousy.

Kaine pulled his fingers from inside her and quickly took her into his strong arms and molded his hard body to hers like a smoothly fitted glove. He hugged her with understanding, "It is okay." His voice, calm, quiet, the voice with no edges now meant to comfort. Kaine gently smoothed the back of her head as he stroked her hair while pushing her cheek against his chest. But his hands no longer hungrily roamed her body.

Damn! She released his full size and wrapped her arms around his waist.

He held her close, dropping an occasional kiss on the top of her head. He took a breath and confessed. "I can tell you this. I never want to be kissed by anyone else the rest of my life."

His words, shot like thunderbolts struck a bulls-eye in the center of her heart of hearts.

"I need you too ... I've never ..." She stopped, not knowing how to tell him never to stop touching her, kissing her, stroking her. Her frustration peaked. She'd never begged to make love yet all he would do was hold her tight.

What was it with Englishmen?

Holly listened to Kaine speak from the hollow of his cheek, admiring his chin sporting a day's growth of dark beard while he questioned her.

"Are you trying to tell me this entire experience is new to you?"

"I'm saying I've never showered with a man. Any intimate experience, I've had, is limited, and a long time ago. I've been alone for so long, seems like forever, and I don't want to disappoint you."

She watched the effect her words had on him as she stroked the line of his jaw. Holly sensed she touched something deep inside Kaine.

His dreamy blue eyes, so genteel were telling her he would take it easy. In a husky, sexy voice, "You, My Lady, could never disappoint me. Your honesty does touch a place in me, I've never known. Your words are stealing my heart, dear lady — and no one's ever done that."

He took a deep, ragged breath and continuing to whisper, "Disappoint me? Never. Keep doing exactly what you are doing. I love your gentle touch, its light, and loving, and makes me feel special, and no one's ever made me feel like that."

Kaine stretched, arching his back, pressing his hard fullness against her belly. He watched her and spoke with gentleness. "I can't make love to you straightaway, not like this. These are your moments to become used to the hard and soft, the taste, and the scent of me. I want you comfortable with the differences between you and me, and then the sameness. Next it will be my turn to learn about you. When you're ready, I promise to ravish you."

Kaine brought his lips down forcefully, searing her mouth to his. He kissed her until she moaned so deep in her throat, her knees melted and gave way.

As he held her up tightly, Holly whispered his name. She opened her dazed eyes, to sink into Kaine's, as he opened his at the same time and locked onto hers.

His breathy words flowed. "I see your eyes say you want me. I choose to wait until they say you love me."

Love him. He wanted her in love with him. Was he crazy too?

Holly thought to comment.

But Kaine kissed her again, passionately, consumed with a raw, primitive love, leaving her aching for him.

Kaine pulled away first and showered her with compliments. "My Lady, you're so loving and desirable." He dropped his wet, pliant lips upon her neck that sent shivers to the center of her wet gender as he repeated. "My Lady." Kaine's hands respectfully caressed Holly's shoulder and returned to her hold her cheeks where he kissed her, first one way then the other.

Her mind was spinning out of control. His words made no sense. He won't make love to me until I say I love him. What was she supposed to do with this burning agony? She cursed herself for lacking the experience to convince him she might love him, maybe even hopelessly loved him since the first moment she'd kissed him. Her eyes were stinging as she fought back tears of despair.

He sensed her change in attitude because Kaine stopped kissing her to say. "Holly?" Alarm laced his voice. "Are you all right?"

Could she explain? "No, no, I don't think I am all right." She grasped a tight hold on his neck, and pulled her lips up to his, and between kisses, she emphasized. "I feel so many things for you. Some so new, I don't understand."

Kaine's arms surrounded her waist and back and smothered her face with sweet, so sweet kisses. "No woman has ever spoken to me like this. Your words touch me as I've never been touched before, My Lady. This experience will be new and exciting for both of us." He insisted as his breath slowed to a shallow pant. He pressed his lips to her ear. "That's why I want to wait. I want you to see me and not driven by new passions that could be for anyone who stood here with you. I am a selfish man. I want you for me and me alone."

"You're speaking of Luka?"

"Maybe, maybe not. I've never wanted to make love with any woman as I do with you. But I want your love more. I believe you're the one, lady, the one.... And for you, I can wait."

The one!

Kaine's words of commitment trailed off as his lips once again searched for hers. He groaned and buried his hands in her hair, pulling her closer, kissing her with deliberate strokes. His words faded away as his mouth closed over hers, kissing her — warm, and wet, teaching her of his raging hunger.

Holly ran her hands over every inch of his body she could reach. Determined to memorize the contour of Kaine, because she wasn't sure if he'd ever allow her to touch him like this again.

Meanwhile, Kaine kissed her freely. His kisses and valiant words spoken between each impassioned kiss enticed her to beg him to reconsider. "I've found out what Hell on Earth is ... to hold you in my arms, on fire with passion, and be bound by an oath of promise not to take you."

Chapter Eight

HEAD OVER HEELS

Holly's body shuddered. What was going on, she wondered as a cold stream of water numbed her passion. She watched as Kaine turned off the hot water.

"What are you doing?" She asked incredulously.

"I'm doing what I can to control myself so I can keep my cursed promise to you," He stated flatly, with a twist of irritation. But the misery in his eyes told the real story.

Holly offered a sympathetic smile, secretly relieved to have her passions cooling, and tried to calm her chattering teeth. "I'm an ice cube. I have to get out." She sucked in her bottom lip, trying to control it from quivering.

Kaine quickly hugged her and tenderly teased her.

"Go, you enchantress, before I don't let you." The hot glaze in his eyes testified to the fact she had seconds to flee.

Holly paused, hoping Kaine would reconsider. They locked onto one another's gaze. All, she found, was his resolve. Kaine meant to keep his promise, and he turned to face the icy water.

Holly stepped into the warm, misty room. She listened to

Kaine groan from the chilled water. She heard him laugh, and then hum, and then he was singing "Now That I've Found You."

Holly had dried herself off by the time he'd turned the water off and reached out to grab a towel. She took his hand and suggested. "At least, let me do something for you and dry your chilled body."

Kaine stuck his wet, shaggy-haired head out from behind the curtain. He grinned with a wry smile. "Doesn't that defeat the purpose?"

"You wanted me to get familiar with you." She said and laughed as he stepped into the giant bath towel she had taken the time to heat on the towel bar. He cooed like a freshly powdered baby.

"Let me warm you," she suggested, stroking his body with a towel.

"Do you think this idea is wise?" he asked, his face strained, questioning her temptation.

Holly ignored him and took another towel to pat dry his long legs, back, and front while she studied his magnificent body. Not too muscular, or a powerlifter like the guys back home at the beach. More than ever, she was convinced he was a runner, or maybe lifted a few weights to shape his magnetic chest. Holly stood behind him to dry his back and the vanity light broke through the steamy atmosphere to unveil his chiseled back. What she saw there shocked her deeply. Holly discovered a secret that should have ceased with the dark ages. Long, faded stripes scarred into his flesh. She'd watched enough movies and recognized them. Her fingertips lightly traced one of the long lashes with the towel. They were old, and the scarring made it hard to tell how many. Over a dozen, she would guess. Who could have caused these horrid marks? And why? Overcome with wonderment and then revulsion she thought about when they were fresh. They must have caused him weeks of unimaginable pain, not to mention the emotional scars.

Kaine, realizing what she had found, flinched, and turned away from her.

Holly looked up at Kaine, her eyes heavy with questions. She softly asked, "What happened?"

"Something too ugly to talk about while I'm so happy," he muttered so low she almost missed it. That was it. Kaine brushed off her inquiry.

She would respect his wishes. But he couldn't stop her from contemplating how they had happened. Had Kaine known her, he would have spilled his guts because he had presented a mystery. She would have to have answers, but she pretended the one he gave her was enough.

She circled him to dry his face. She moved easily, her mind preoccupied with questions. Holly paused and dragged her red lacquered thumbnail across his bottom lip. She moved to Kaine's neck, then his chest. As she knelt in front of him to dry his sleeping desire, Kaine caught her elbow and pulled her up to stand beside him.

He raised an arched brow. "I don't think that would be wise." He cautioned as his eyes twinkled, his tone firm.

Holly smiled quickly, but she couldn't shake the dreadful image of his lashes, called scourging during the times of Jesus, flogging during the Buccaneer times, and whipping during the days of the Civil War. However, this was the twentieth century, and called abuse, extreme physical, and emotional abuse. How had this happened to the world's greatest singer? Lost in thought, Holly, had not noticed Kaine slipping on one of the white terry cloth robes.

He held the second out for her. "My turn to pamper you." He offered with a cheerful smile, leaving whatever painful memories of his past, masked behind the smile. "Put this on, you need to wear something before I can't remember what I promised you, My Lady."

His warning producing a new gentleness in his eyes that both surprised and endeared her to him.

As he held the robe open for her, he studied her naked body.

She watched the lust take over his thoughts by the second.

He invited. "Come on...."

She followed Kaine out to the couch.

The logs were coaxing the fire to dance in the hearth, giving off a warm, inviting glow. The dinner cart sat beside the couch. Kaine picked up the silver teapot and poured the amber liquid into the bone china cups. The light aroma of lavender steam rose as if smoke rising from incense.

Holly sat on the end of the couch tucking her feet under her. He served her. She took her teacup and sipped the hot, tangy infusion. Mmmm, everything was perfect. She leaned back listening to Roberts playing softly in the background.

Kaine drank a few gulps before setting his cup down and moved closer to her to ask, "Do you mind if I comb your beautiful hair?"

Holly produced a happy grin to answer his question. He produced the wide toothcomb from his pocket.

Kaine repositioned her and sat behind her, close, oh, so close. He stretched his long legs alongside her the length of the couch. The clean scent of him made her dizzy, so she closed her eyes and choked back her longing to abandon propriety, turn and spread her legs to straddle him.

They sat quietly like long time lovers. Kaine started at the bottom of her hair, parting it into sections. He worked his way to the nape of her neck as if he had done it often.

"Whose hair did you comb before me?" She asked, biting her lip, hoping he didn't think she was prying again.

"My Mom. Her hair was like yours in length, but it was golden hair. Angel's hair, I use to believe as a young boy."

"Blonde? Your father's the one with the dark hair?" Uh, oh. He stiffened. She'd struck a nerve, a painful one by his reaction.

He grunted, "Yeah, I've been told we looked exactly alike."

"He is handsome?"

"Was...."

Before she could stop herself, she blurted, "Was!"

"My father's dead, been years," he stated with a flat, edgy tone that warned her not to ask.

Her curiosity ignored his warning and compelled her to do exactly that. "How did your mother take his death?"

He stiffened again, and with a shaky voice, spoke barely above a whisper, "She died before him."

Holly's heart sank. Orphaned. How awful. Holly clammed up, realizing the moments were hanging heavy, and if she had any hope of restoring the happiness she had been sharing with him, it was time to end her inquiry.

"I'm sorry." He apologized, squeezing her with his knees, and put the comb down beside her.

Holly could have kicked herself. Here she sat with the most desirable man in the world, and she might as well have thrown ice-cold water on him.

Kaine got up and moved into his bedroom.

She sat alone with her self-doubt inspecting his beautiful guitars, and Roberts' fiery, slow hand, called to her from the CD player. She couldn't resist and picked up the vintage acoustic guitar and strummed a few of the chords she recognized Roberts playing. She hadn't realized Kaine had returned composed, lifted the Stratocaster, and was playing lead to mesh with her rhythm chords.

Holly smiled a weak smile, so sorry she had caused him any discomfort.

Kaine broke the silence and asked, "How long have you played guitar?"

She noticed the earlier sparkle had returned to his eyes, and hoped that meant he was ready to forgive her intrusion into his mysterious past, so she answered, "Since I was a kid. I don't consider myself a guitar player. I played enough to keep up with my father and accompany myself when I scratch out a song."

"Brilliant! You write songs?" He exclaimed excitedly as his eyes brighten.

And Holly was quickly learning that when Kaine's face sparkled there was no better feeling for her. "Of sorts. It's been a while, mostly thoughts. Helps me relax. Dad plays to relax. He still talks about the time he met John Roberts during the sixties in San Francisco. He'd sat in with John at a jam session. Roberts' his favorite."

"Mine as well." Kaine conceded.

She'd known that. There were many things she intuitively

understood about this nomadic stranger. How vividly she could picture her Dad sitting on his special rock overlooking the Pacific Ocean with Kaine perched beside him, two old souls talking to each other connecting by playing guitars. Yes, her Dad would positively love Kaine.

Kaine impulsively requested. "I'd like to meet your father someday."

Holly sat stunned, thinking he had read her mind, but beyond that, Kaine had plans to keep her around for a while. "I'd like that." She admitted with ease and returned to the guitar. She hesitated and decided to add. "My father will adore you."

Kaine glanced over at her as he continued to pick a beautiful scale. "I hope I have the same effect on his daughter." He countered and grinned.

His words sang to her heart. Kaine was simply too charming. Holly took note of him draped in his white robe. His long damp hair spread about his shoulders like a black cape. The days' growth of beard on his face made her forget her father, and her past because he was so damn gorgeous.

She came alive. The blood was rushing through her veins and wicked thoughts flowed, causing her to swell. And overcome the temptation to strip him of the robe, and make love then and there, she wanted to scream at him. I love you, I love you, and I love you. There I've said it — make me forget you ever made your silly promise.

But something stopped her from saying the words aloud. Instead, she sat and played the beautiful guitar, thinking how different this man was from the man on the stage, from the man in the video. Kaine the man, she was beginning to see — the real man.

The Roberts song ended and Kaine set down his guitar and headed for the dinner cart. He turned and offered. "Champagne?"

Holly wasn't in the mood. Champagne was for a celebration, and she had lost the sensual flow of yearning. So she half-smiled and asked, "May I have a beer?"

"You, My Lady, are a woman after my own heart." He declared popping the bottle cap.

"You're right Kaine. I am after your heart." She teased.

He smiled one of his endearing smiles, flashing his dimples to her. "To you, I give it freely."

His mood had changed, and Kaine didn't seem to be teasing. He brought her beer. She took a swig and sat it down, taken aback by his mineral water. Where was his beer? Holly thought to change her mind, but what the hell. It was only beer.

Kaine picked up his guitar and sat next to her on the couch while Roberts started a new song.

Holly absent-mindedly pulled the guitar closer to her and leaned on Kaine. Holly plucked and strummed the strings, accompanying Kaine while occasionally smiling to each other, especially in those moments when they hit and played in sync. Coming after a shared moment, she casually asked, "Who was the man following us today?"

"Following us?"

"In my line of work, I notice these things." She casually pointed out.

Kaine continued to play, his voice even. "What might that be that you notice people following us? Don't tell me you're a reporter. Or with the CIA or British Intelligence? No, you couldn't tell me if you were a spy, let me see."

She saw the teasing in his eyes. "Nothing so covert, I work at a criminal law firm and I often research clients. Occasionally, it takes me into the field where I do light surveillance. So, naturally, I'd notice a man following us."

Kaine didn't look up but informed her nonchalantly. "I instructed my bodyguard to stay as far away from me ... I meant us, as far as security would allow. It might have been him, or an overzealous fan or a reporter. It's not unusual for me to be followed."

"I forget how famous you are. I had never heard of you before last night."

Kaine's face instantly spread with surprise and dropped his chin to his chest.

At once, she wished she hadn't allowed her words. She gingerly put the guitar down and expressed her regret. "I'm sorry. I should keep my big mouth shut. To explain, I've heard of the band, of course, seen a few old videos and loved some of your songs. But you ... I'm sorry."

Kaine followed her lead, leaning his guitar against the couch. He didn't move.

Suddenly, he lunged at her, grabbing her by the waist and pulled her down to the floor.

At a loss for what to think or do, she laid pinned solid under the length of his weight, taken aback by his spontaneous response.

Kaine peered down at her. His hair fell forward and he joyously responded. "You, My Lady, are the best thing that's happened to me in a long time. It's so refreshing to meet someone who hasn't heard of me and rambles off all my accomplishments as if I wasn't present. You seriously never heard of me?" He prompted, with a tiny, noticeable hurt tone and added, "How the bloody hell did you win?"

"My assistant, she entered me into the contest so I could win a well-deserved vacation to London," she explained, so sorry, her answer was matter-of-fact. She didn't want to tell him she'd mainly accepted the award to escape Brett.

Holly watched his face grow more confused. Quick to explain more, Holly continued.

"It took a while to place the name. The band's reputation was well let's say discouraging at best, with all the negative press over the past decade. Last night's concert refreshed my memory. I'd been singing your songs for years. I'd never put the song titles, and you the singer in Hurrikaine, as the same, poor research on my part. I am sorry ... I hope I haven't offended you?"

"No ... never, I love it. So, you have no idea of what I've done, or where I've been?"

"I know you are a kind and gentle man by the lyrics you have written. I can only assume that by this lavish suite, your success has afforded you the eccentric lifestyle of a rock star. Not one I would envy because it must be so difficult to be you. No matter. I'm glad to be here with you in spite of your profession."

Kaine lets go with a boisterous laugh, pushed himself off her, and lay beside her. He pulled her face close, so close that she wished to move to him and kiss his sweet-scented lips. Instead, his lips moved along her neck and between soft kisses, he admitted.

"I have had people tell me my entire career they wanted to

be me. Tonight I am with a woman who does not envy my life and thinks it's difficult to be me."

Kaine stopped and dove deep into her eyes.

She melted under his charm.

His eyes said he was serious.

"My Lady, it's exceedingly difficult to be me — next to fucking impossible to be me. I've been alone so long trying to find 'me.' I've become so isolated from the world it's pathetic. They all say look there goes the famous Kaine. They forget, I am Kaine Walker, a man first. But I've found out the hard way that my accomplishments mean little when I can't share them with someone special."

His confession was a surprise, like him, Kaine the man was different. Her stomach tighten, and she placed her arms around his neck to comfort him, pulled his face close to hers again, and reminded.

"I know Kaine, the man. I know his lips."

And she kissed his lips lightly.

"I know his neck."

And she kissed his neck up and down the smooth column until she was pleased with raising trails of tiny bumps.

"I know his chest."

And she kissed it, spending a great deal of time.

"I know his legs."

And her hand reached down under his robe to stroke his leg upward. She moved her hand higher to the top of his thigh, coming dangerously close to resting her fingers near the mystery of him.

"I know you, Kaine. My heart and soul know you. And like the song you sang at the Hard Rock, now that I've found you,

you're not alone anymore."

"Holly, please. Show me a bit of mercy," Kaine begged as he bolted up taking her shoulders in his hands and pushing her away.

"You can't talk this way. Not tonight." He paused and grabbed a hearty breath.

"Soon, My Lady, soon, I will make love to you."

Chapter Nine

SPEND MY LIFE

Holly lay listening to the bold patterns of the evening's rainstorm as the sheets of water pounded relentlessly on the suite's windows, warning her to stay put for the night. The evening with Kaine was not turning out as she'd imagined. Holly dreamed her next lover would be gregarious, ravishing her until she could scarcely catch her breath. She never counted on another English gentleman.

Holly watched Kaine, as he walked toward her. She wanted to reach out, and stroke his leg, which kept escaping from his robe with each stride. The closer he came, the more she realized that these few days would not be enough to quench her increasing appetite for him.

Kaine nudged her to sit next to her. He placed her between his legs and invited her to lean back on his chest and joked.

"I can hold you in my arms without compromising either of us." A boyish smile wrapped around his lips.

She scooted back and leaned against him. His arms folded around her waist, careful not to touch her breasts. Holly snuggled into his body, savoring his warmth, drenched with his hypnotizing scent while they relaxed on the couch quietly listening to Roberts and the rain. Occasionally his lips would press into her neck, sending quiet quakes of tenderness rippling through her heart. One of his hands slipped inside her robe to stroke her lower abdomen.

After a while, Kaine twisted and sucked in a breath.

She sensed this was something she did not want to hear.

He kissed her neck and nibbled her earlobe.

She bristled in response.

He measured each word carefully. "Holly, I can't think of anything I'd rather do, well ...."

Yes, of course. Since his cursed promise, to make love was all either of them could think about doing.

He stammered as if taking his time, deciding how to say what was on his mind.

She turned to see him lower his magnificent long dark lashes. What could be bothering him?

"I've never needed to say this before meeting you," he explained in a hurry. "Please understand. The kinds of women I am used to aren't virgins. Most are barely a step up from an alley cat. The majority don't come with a name, and if they do, I don't remember."

Holly bolted up to turn to question him, but Kaine kept his arms tightly around her, securing her to his body.

"Please, hear me out. I ... I've been tested. I have none of the sexually transmitted diseases, and I'm HIV negative. I'm telling you all this because it's important to your future. I need you to trust me when I say I have been alone for a long time, by choice."

He hesitated a moment.

His lungs fill with air.

"... about protection, we will need to agree how to handle ... well, you are special to me, and I wouldn't want anything unplanned to happen to you. Understand?" Kaine's asked as he pressed his warm, bristly, cheek against hers.

She was glad he was sitting behind her so Kaine couldn't see her cheeks wearing the searing embarrassment. But as always, she had questions. "Why have you stayed alone? You're on top of the world and can pick any woman you want."

"Perhaps that is why. Something that is plentiful becomes a bore after a while."

"How are you sure ... you want me?" She countered, in a tiny voice that was losing volume by the second.

"The moment I saw you. You were different with Luka, and then with me. You didn't look at me as if you'd discovered the Pope. It was something in your eyes that said you had a chance to see the real me. After all, of our talks, at the risk of sounding arrogant, I'm convinced you could truly love me, Kaine Walker.

"Another reason is you don't have the hard rock music facade to stand between you and me. You also don't have the haughtiness I see in women attempting to impress me. Or, seem to need to make a name for yourself due to an association with me. You're honest and sincere, and both are rare qualities in rock music.

"You didn't care who the hell I was to impress you. My ego can take a battering, but it was about the way you gave yourself to me during the video. It was as if you trusted your whole life to me ... as if you needed me. Few people truly need me. Most of the world needs my money and fame — not me.

"If none of those are the reason. Then your kiss ... you are the only woman to kiss me so lovingly. There was no thought in my mind to take you to bed. To do things I've done with so many women. I couldn't think of anything but your sweetness. I wanted to stay there holding you, kissing you for eternity," he explained and relaxed his hold on her.

She turned around to gaze into his beautiful Technicolor blue eyes that promised he'd meant every word he'd said.

"Holly, I'm not sure if I've made any sense because it was on the heels of your incredible kiss that my lustful thoughts crowded my mind. But Holly, for those few seconds we stood together, I couldn't find where I stopped, and you began. I've never felt so complete, so whole — ever."

Kaine moved in and pressed his lips to hers again, urgently as if to remind him, she was not a dream. He pulled back barely allowing his tongue to trace the outline of her closed lips.

"Something in me has changed. Here with you makes me forget where I come from, who I am but mostly makes me think about who I want to become with you."

On the heels of his powerful confession, she moved closer, tilting her head to open her mouth, and kiss him deeply to show him she agreed in every way. But he pushed her away. He was driving her nuts.

Kaine's eyes locked onto hers, searching them, saying he hoped she felt the same.

Stunned into silence, she failed to convince him she agreed with his assessment. She saw her silence was causing him concern because his expression tensed, and his eyebrows became pensive. But she was stunned silent because his words had deeply flooded her empty heart.

He added, "I plan to have you to love for a long, long time."

Kaine's words cut deeper into her heart of hearts, his poet's words, to have you to love for a long, long time.

Holly cuddled into his chest. "What if I want the beginning of this journey of love to start with you tonight?" She challenged, recapturing her senses, gaining strength as the moments passed.

Kaine sat back quietly. So long, she thought she had offended him.

After a long moment, he pensively surrendered. "I've never met a woman like you. I want to kiss you madly, touch you and love you. Still, something inside me says stop. Wait."

His soulful blue eyes locked onto hers, and he quietly cautioned. "Soon ... I'll show you how aroused I am. I haven't started to drive your body crazy."

Spellbound once more by his charming outburst, Holly leaned into Kaine's arms and almost swooned. Holly lingered as Kaine kissed her hair.

Out of the blue, he sat up straight and moved her off him declaring, "I have to get up, or you'll suffer the consequences. I can only be responsible for so long." Kaine walked over to his guitar, picked it up, and strummed a few chords. Distracted by Roberts, he turned the volume down on the CD player, grabbed a pencil and hurriedly scratched words on a piece of paper.

She sat quietly for a long time watching the toast of London, listening to his perfect voice sing fragments of lyrics, the voice with no edges.

Holly drifted.

"Holly, Holly ... My Lady," he questioned. "Where are

you?"

She was thinking about how it was time for her to leave and go back to her hotel room. Luka shouldn't be a problem because it was after one in the morning. His manners would prevent him from calling her at that hour. Holly stood up and asserted in a smooth but firm voice.

"Kaine, its best I go back to my hotel."

Kaine stopped playing and quickly set down the guitar. "I thought you promised you would not leave me?" He grumbled. His facial expression covered with a cloud of anguish. "You're safe here. I keep my promises."

"It's me, Kaine. I can't stay here with you with all these new emotions."

Kaine rushed to her side, taking her hand in his and pleaded. "Holly, how many times must I tell you? I've never wanted a woman as badly as I do you ... this moment. You do, believe me?"

Holly stood back, and she smiled half-heartily. She understood the feelings all too well. No wedding night would be sweeter. However, she hoped if they stayed on this course he would not make her wait that long.

But what was this?

Kaine stepped away, pulling her by the hand, leading her toward the bedroom. He turned off the lights as he left the living room, and then in the bedroom.

Holly stood in the inky darkness. Kaine lets go of her hand. She heard his robe hit the floor and the sound of the crisp sheets rustling beneath him.

"I can't promise I can do this, but I will try. Come, lay beside me, and try to sleep. You must be crashing from the jetlag, and I have to work early today, and I need to rest if I can."

How could she say no to his invitation to lay and rest with him? She silently agreed by dropping her robe and slid into paradise where her body was a perfect fit with his.

Kaine's warm hands circled her waist, and he held her close, oh, so close.

She listened to Kaine's heart pounding as if about to burst. Holly thought she'd go deaf counting the beats of his heart, in the middle of the queen-sized bed, where he no longer slept alone.

Chapter Ten

CAN'T GET ENUFF

Day 3

olly opened her eyes to greet the rising sun. She felt overwhelmed by Kaine's unusual behavior, yet filled with happiness from his charming confessions making it difficult to sleep.

She thought to nestle her body up against Kaine's warm — what. She glanced over to find a pile of pillows separating her from the honorable Kaine hell-bent on honoring his promise. Apparently, sometime during the night, he'd built a pillow barrier between them. Her disappointment rose quickly, yet she couldn't stop the smile from curling around her lips. She leaned over the mountain of fluff stacked to keep his promise. She knew she faced the beautiful man. She was falling in love with him.

The sun's golden rays streamed in through a crack in the drapes as the golden bars of light majestically crowned Kaine's head and spread to accentuate his perfectly sculptured face. Holly draped herself across the tower of pillows, wondering how long she would be this happy. She reached out to touch his sun-kissed arm, so pale against his dark body hair, wishing she had awoken peacefully wrapped in his trustworthy embrace. Although she was pleased that the temptation of her made him pull away, she longed for the flesh-and-blood of him.

Kaine was quietly sleeping. His closed eyes appeared as dark crescents dressed with long, dark lashes that rested against the ridge of his cheeks. Spread on the stark white sheet was his long, dark, tousled locks she loved to curl about her fingers. His exquisite, peaceful face, deep in sleep, mesmerized her. His breathing was quiet, deep, measured, and she wanted to kiss his long sleek neck. Instead, she delicately brushed his chest with her fingertips careful not to awaken her sleeping prince.

Locked in those precious moments, Holly realized she had never awakened next to a naked man. How many of life's simple joys had she missed? She stifled the opportunity to lift the sheet wrapped protectively around his thighs to peek, remembering the full size of him pressing against her in the shower. She imagined how she would enjoy him growing by her touch. Mostly, she daydreamed about how truly happy he would make her when he was a full size inside her, making all her fantasies come true.

Suddenly, his private cellular phone, on the nightstand rang loud and intrusive, jarring Holly's thoughts. Was there no escape? Seconds later, it rang again.

No, movement.

The caller wouldn't give up and rang a third time. Kaine stirred — slightly.

Again, the persistent ringing. With his right hand, Kaine reached out, stretching over her as a cat. He grabbed the phone, brought it to him and pulled the antenna as far as it allowed and placed it to his ear.

"Yeah, speak."

There was silence from Kaine, other than occasional grunts acknowledging, or agreeing with the intruder.

He broke the silence and confirmed. "No problem. Lady's with me."

Holly perked up, who would look for her here? Who the hell in London knew she would be with Kaine Walker rock star?

Kaine laid down beside Holly pulling her into him and handed her the phone. "An admirer." He indicated as he motioned with his head for her to take the receiver.

She didn't like the sound of that, so she reluctantly took it feeling so — caught.

"Hello," she grumbled.

"Good morning. Sleep well?" His tone was cold.

She heard his disappointment behind the question.

She responded briskly, in a condemned tone. "Luka...."

The phone was silent — dead.

"I don't know what to say?" Holly managed as a tight twisting of guilt instantly reached out to strangle her. She knew enough of Luka's history, hurting from a tragic past, and yet yesterday, he'd taken a big step, wondering if he could start again with her. She was ashamed at how badly she'd abused his burgeoning trust. "Luka," she repeated below her breath, under Kaine's watchful stare.

"I thought you were a sensible woman. You can fool

yourself, but I bloody well know Kaine." Luka reprimanded, his voice so cold and sharp, she barely recognized him.

"It's not what you think." It wasn't. She had only slept with him — nothing more, nothing less — well maybe a bit more.

"How do you know what I think? I know Kaine. Tell me if I'm correct. Somehow, he invited you to his hotel room for dinner. Promised nothing more?"

The long strangling fingers of betrayal started to choke her. She glanced at Kaine. She watched the muscle in his cheek twitch and his eyes were watching her, piercing her, saying so much, telling her to hang up the phone.

Luka was spot on with his poisoned remark. That was how everything had happened, the rain, his promise, and dinner.

"You don't have to answer. I can tell by your silence you fell for his oldest trick."

"Luka, please don't say those things. You don't understand."

Kaine pressed her harder, and his piercing blue eyes urged her to get off the phone.

She was in an unbearable position.

"Don't try to explain. It's only a matter of time. I can tell by your attitude — I'm too late. If you'd listened to me …"

She watched the expression on Kaine's face slipping in, and out of jealousy. Their night — the innocence — his promise to her. Had he made a colossal fool of her? Had she made a terrible mistake?

Luka was speaking again, and she strained to hear him over her swirling thoughts.

"If Kaine steps out of line, tell me. He's not what you think he is. Anyway, last night's history. If it's important, I rang you last night, again this morning to meet for breakfast. When they told me you hadn't returned, it wasn't difficult to find you. Please, believe me. I'm not ringing to check on you."

Holly tried to ignore the disappointment lacing his voice over her choice of bed partners.

Kaine cuddled up close, attempting to distract her. It wasn't working. She couldn't respond to Kaine. Luka might as well be in the room with them — watching.

Kaine didn't care. He lightly stroked her body below her belly, sending tiny chills to run rampantly. He lingered as his hair hung long, brushing along her body. He placed his warm, moist mouth on the curve of her breast. Ummm, his warm lips, so delicious against her cool skin. Her thoughts were blocked, and she couldn't hear whatever it was Luka was going on about as if he had her full attention.

"Why have you called at sunrise?" She interrupted with a firm edge, hoping to appease him and get off the damn phone. The heat that was shooting up her body insisted she deal with Kaine. Now!

"It's not that early." Luka spewed and insisted.

"Listen to me. We need to get this day started. Kaine is due at Briarwood Castle in a few hours for the last of the video shoot. I finished running the film footage shot yesterday. You both were brilliant! So hot, CMT has requested, no, demanded I put you into today's shoot. Your involvement is not a guest shot. I'm talking money, big money for a few hours of work. Interested?"

Interested. Big money? CMT would pay her big money to be with Kaine. How had this happened? A few hours ago, she would have happily shot an epic with him for free. Still, she had some pride, and she hesitated, it would mean she would be on location with both Luka and Kaine. How wise a move was that? And she didn't like to be suspicious about Luka's motives, but by the determined sound of his voice, Luka wouldn't let her leave with Kaine as easily the second time.

"Holly? If I have any influence left, do the shoot — for me?"

The last time he had asked her to do something for him she had worn a black lace dress, and enchanted Kaine. What would be in store for her this time?

Kaine's dark-haired head nuzzled her breasts, reclaiming her attention as his warm tongue tantalized her sensitive skin, raising bumps as he circled the globe of first one breast then the other.

"Well?" Luka stated pointedly.

Kaine's oldest trick, indeed?

His impaling words had cast dispersions on her budding love for Kaine, seriously tarnishing her trust. Again, Kaine pressed his warm, succulent lips against the mountainous curves of her breast.

This lusty predicament was Hell.

What to do next?

Chapter Eleven

TANGLED IN THE WEB

Today's challenge — to decide if she should venture out with these two powerhouse Englishmen, or to stay behind at her hotel and choose a sightseeing tour of London.

Putting her decision in perspective, she released a shallow breath and asked Luka, "Please, hold for a moment."

"Kaine, Luka's asking me to do a video shoot at the castle. I wouldn't usually ask, however, considering these unusual circumstances, what are your thoughts on spending another day together?"

"Luka's already brought me up to speed. I can't think of a better place to have a second date. But this decision is up to you, so you'll have to follow your heart, My Lady."

Some help he was, except the curious way he'd called the video shoot a date. She was dating Kaine Walker, the rock superstar!

She turned back to Luka and stressed her need for complete disclosure. "What is it you expect from me at the shoot? I can't handle any surprises this time."

Luka grunted something unintelligible.

She wished it were his sweet, joyous laugh.

Kaine returned to entertain himself by caressing her body with long, meaningful strokes, reminding her of where she was as he latched onto one of her hardened nipples. He wasn't dedicated to either as he turned his body, placing his head on her lap. He lavished attention first on one breast, then the other, lingering, kissing, sucking, and licking longer than she'd ever dreamed possible.

She barely heard Luka saying.

"I see the position you're in Babe."

Did he.

"It is bad form on Kaine's part," he complained. "As you can see he can't be trusted. He's not a gentleman, not in his blood. Hate to admit it, but I do agree with his intuition yesterday at the video shoot. He was on the bleedin' money this time. The footage will surprise you. It's smashing! That brings us to today. I need you to ride on the back of a horse, behind Kaine. It will take a large part of the day, and I'm up against time because the bloody clouds are threatening to storm straightaway. But you can count on a full day."

Luka stopped, and in a small, quiet voice said, "In case you're speculating. I won't cause you any problems. You'll have enough with Kaine. Remember, I'm here, close by if you need me. So, can I count on you?" He probed, ever the businessman with an edge of challenge in his voice.

Holly squirmed under the ferocious and fiery touch of Kaine, unable to repress a wicked smile. This was becoming a true fairy tale with all the trimmings. Until Luka's biting words cut deep and fractured her fairy tale.

He's not a gentleman.
Not in his blood.
Can't be trusted.

Holly pulled herself together. She fought Kaine's focused attention, pushed at him, and squirmed to pull up the sheet between them. She couldn't look into his eyes, not yet. Flashes of memories with Luka burst into her mind invading her pleasures with Kaine. It was supposed to have been her and Luka's fairy tale, to live happily ever after. Instead, Kaine had stepped into her life out of the mist. He'd brought a kiss so magical, she'd forgotten her beautiful angel and any promise of a future. Well, she would have to do something to smooth the waters. Luka was back, and he seemingly understood her predicament. She considered Kaine's reaction, watching him resting beside her, stretched out long, and languid, his facial expression flooding with confusion.

"Yes, I'll do the shoot. Thank you Luka, for the offer." She politely added, almost choking on her decision, wondering if she was making another colossal mistake.

Appeased, Luka continued, his voice sounded warmer, and the tension between them seemed less strained. "Brilliant. Oh, and save your thanks. You're the irresistible one. And when you get around to ordering breakfast, scan the newspapers. You might be interested in a couple of pieces."

Luka had a way of capturing her curiosity and now was no exception.

"What is it, Luka?"

"I'll let you find them, but back to business. The car will be at the hotel in an hour. We need all the light we can capture, so get Kaine dressed straightaway. Will ya?" Luka pushed, and his tone twisted with an edge of disgust.

Holly wished that Luka would stop with all the insinuations. But again, he knew Kaine, perhaps too well. She couldn't think about that any longer. Luka had caught her, and she would try to explain to him later that nothing had happened. Then, Luka already knew that, didn't he?

"Don't worry, we'll be ready," she assured.

The suite's phone rang a second time before she could get out of bed.

Kaine finally gave in and answered. Seconds later, he spoke only one word with a guarded restraint. "No." He slammed the phone down, turned, lunged, and playfully grabbed at her. He wrapped his body around hers, and kissed her ear. "Looks like you're of interest to the tabloids. That was a reporter friend of mine wanting me to name my mysterious girlfriend. Seems a well-meaning fan saw me kissing you in front of the palace and snapped a shot. We're on the cover of The Daily Sun with a sketchy story about my secret girlfriend."

Kaine paused, studying her seriously. "Understand, this situation is different. I've never had a girlfriend after the first date. In fact, I haven't had a girlfriend in many years so this headline will change us fast. I can't adjust my life. I'm contractually obligated for the next eighteen months, and the pace is in the fast lane. So this will be the first of many decisions we can make together. Or if you have any sense, you'll get out now — while you can," he challenged, staring her straight in the eyes.

Holly wondered what to make of his preposterous speech.

"First date. Girlfriend. I'm not sure what you are telling me Kaine, and you are scaring me."

"What I'm telling you is, we met yesterday. In the space of twenty-four hours, we went from strangers to going on our first date, to the public believing you are my secret girlfriend. And because we don't know each other at all like our personal histories, our favorite foods, and movies, or, how I have kept a promise that stopped us from more than sleeping together. We have been thrown together in the spotlight as lovers. No matter what I say to the media unless you leave me today, they believe us to be a couple. So, with little information to make such an important decision, you have to decide if I am what you want." He pointed out with an edge of shyness in his eyes.

His explanation frightened her more than confuse her. Did he want her to leave him today because of this dramatic turn of events?

"I didn't understand that last night was a date. What about Luka?" She pushed herself even closer to him and tightly wrapped her arms around him. "Kaine, I'm not sure what you are asking of me?"

"Luka knows Holly. Remember, he is the one that encouraged you to accept my invitation. My Lady, didn't you realize I'd asked you out — to go sightseeing and to dinner? Where I come from that is a date, a romantic date. Things are starting to move incredibly fast, and won't stop for a while.

"So you understand my intentions. It has been about five years since I've had a woman around long enough to care for, be with, wake up and spend the day together. I'm asking you, what do you want me to tell the press? Are we only friends? Or do you want to stay with me, and play out this hand fate has dealt to us? I'm hoping you say yes, but the question is, do you want to be known as Kaine Walker's girlfriend?"

Holly lay stunned in his arms. Too much had happened in such a short amount of time to sort out any feelings. She had met Luka merely a few days ago, and they were going to start a love affair, and look how that worked out. Twenty-four hours later, Luka passed her to Kaine. They'd gone on a date apparently condoned by all parties, except her. Now she had to choose if she wanted to commit to a permanent relationship with an entirely different man. And this amazing, and an elegant man lying next to her hoped she'd say yes because the press was pushing.

So, how did she feel?

Was this rational?

Was this sensible?

Was it even real?

How was she supposed to close up her life in L.A., and stay with Kaine Walker, superstar — just like that?

What was real?

Kaine was asking her to go on a journey of a lifetime with him. He'd confessed to wanting her and would take her with him. Most people lived the course of their lives never taking a chance. They never put themselves in a position where they could find true happiness. And especially because he was a rock star, she should absolutely say no. But it was a man named Kaine, she wanted. And it was he that was asking her to stay. There was only one answer to his question.

"I'm as confused as you are from this quick turn of events. With so little to base a reasonable decision on other than this blinding attraction and longing for each other, I can't see myself walking away. Hold my hand tight Kaine and take me with you. Show me all the ways I can make your life better, how to care for you, how to love you. I'm willing to do what it takes to make a commitment work with you. I agree, this twist of fate is an incredible hand dealt to us, and I can't see letting it pass. So, I will trust you. It would be an honor to be known as Kaine Walker's girlfriend for as long as you want me."

His face softened showing his million-dollar smile, hugged by his bracketed dimples.

Holly stared back flattered, yet astounded — just like that — the dream man was hers. Hmm, the choice seemed too easy. The decision made. She looked at Kaine she was his girlfriend. She couldn't stop the wicked smile forming on her lips.

"So that's why Luka advised me to scan the newspapers."

"That's it. Forget Luka, you, My Lady, have made me exceptionally happy. I will do my best to keep my promise and protect you from the severities in my world. It will come at you hard and fast. But I believe that you are the one that will stay close to me. There are hundreds of details we must sort soon, but for now, it's time. Come with me, girlfriend. We have to get ready for our second date." He released a small chuckle accepting the twist in his fate. His face radiated his complete joy and happiness because she would stay with him.

Kaine pulled her as close as possible, and he gazed into her eyes for the longest moment. It was as if he was willing her all the strength she would need to be his lady. He closed his eyes and with his soft lips, he brushed her mouth ever so slightly but did not press to enter. He lovingly held her and took a breath, sighed and released her. He rolled out of the bed and playfully whacked her exposed fanny.

"Ouch." She cried out in jest as she picked up a pillow and hurled it at him.

Kaine scooted quickly across the carpet toward the bath, laughing at her poor aim.

She closed her eyes to avoid staring at his secret area, why torture herself unnecessarily?

"Isn't my new girlfriend going to help me steam up the shower? It's part of the job description," Kaine pointed out, poking his head out the bathroom door, so delighted with the news.

"Not on your life. We'll be late," she replied. Her tone turned more serious. "You grab a quick shower, and I'll call room service for breakfast. When you're finished, I'll shower alone if you don't mind. I need to do something about my clothes. They're probably ruined. I forgot all about them and left them in a pile."

"Closets yours. Anything that is mine is yours." He pointed across the room. "Pick what you want. But you're missing a great shower," he encouraged to coax her in with him.

"I'm totally aware of what I'm missing. And you are wrong, it's better than great," she agreed and blew him a kiss.

Holly stretched out on his bed to work the kinks out of her tense muscles. A second date. She had to laugh, their second date, and already Kaine's girlfriend. And Luka knew. What must he think and feel? But Luka had the answers, knew all too well how this fast pace world worked.

But why had he sent her into Kaine's waiting arms, knowing what would happen. Because if this was Kaine's former method of operation, judging by what Kaine had told her, he hadn't been picking up girlfriends lately. She wondered if the headline took Luka by surprise.

She decided she must put Luka out of her mind, for now,

she was with Kaine and she would deal with Mr. Hunter later. Next, she had to contend with Brett. Since her initial confusion had faded, she wasn't sure how long it would take the news on the front page of newspapers to reach Brett. She was officially Kaine Walker's secret girlfriend, and he seemed jubilant with the notion.

Girlfriend... Anything that is mine is yours ...

Everything was moving way too fast.

She got up, called room service, and placed an order. The cold air blanketing her naked body was invigorating. She wandered into Kaine's closet, drawing in a deep whiff of his alluring scent. She selected a pair of his leather patched Levi's and a crimson, silk shirt. A wide, black leather belt would work for her waist. The fire should have dried out her heels. She turned around to lay them on his bed. When she glanced up, she found him standing in the doorway, clean-shaven, hair wet and combed straight back, loosely wrapped in the white terry cloth robe, about his tall, lean frame. He was positively the most elegant man on earth, perhaps in the universe. Kaine's darling blue eyes fixed upon her.

"Well, well, My Lady. You are a beauty to look at." He praised while he folded his arms across his chest and leaned in the doorway.

She heard him sigh under his breath.

"All the better to please you with, My Lord," she pledged, in a sultry voice as she slipped past him in the doorway, close, oh, so close. As she passed, she stole a mint scented kiss from him.

Holly adjusted the temperature of the shower water thinking he had left to dress in the bedroom. She tested the water, flung her long hair over her shoulder, and was about to enter the mist when she caught Kaine in her peripheral vision. He was still staring at her, apparently hypnotized by her. She smiled to herself and stood proudly. She stretched, posing, allowing him to admire her feminine shape for a long moment, and stepped into the misty water.

After her shower, Kaine was missing. She continued into the living room to find him in a conversation on the phone. The breakfast cart had arrived. He winked at her, covered the mouthpiece, gestured toward the cart with his head, and responded to his caller.

"That's right. Make it happen." He hesitated. "That's better."

He walked toward Holly wearing a long-sleeved, red-and-white checked, flannel shirt, tucked into stonewashed Levi's and black and white alligator boots. His damp hair fell loosely about his beautiful face. To add to that delicious sight of him, the fresh scent of his cologne sent a wake-up call to stoke her desire.

Oh, no. Not that again. Surely, she would never stop feeling this way.

As she selected a slice of cantaloupe, and asked, "What are the plans, Kaine?"

He moved behind her and slipped his arms around her waist, and his hands disappeared inside her robe. He fondled the tips of her breasts with his thumbs sending chills all over her body. "Mmmm, you smell great." He said with a sexy tone as he turned her and moved his hands on around to her back, bringing her into his arms, and tightly hugged her. "It's not any easier to keep my promise by the light of day, especially given our new relationship."

Holly peered over his shoulder. She caught sight of his reflection in the mirror across from her. His face was braided with a wicked grin.

"Is that what you call keeping your promise while I was trying to talk to Luka on the phone?" She grinned because her body was heating up incredibly fast due to his masterful and feisty touch.

"Yes, My Lady, but have I not remained honorable? I have only sampled the forbidden fruit. And it is sweet. I hunger until the time I can love thou the way I was intended." He risked in his best Shakespearean voice as if to tease her.

Kaine succeeded in making her laugh, and his gallant words fueled a heady love. They both knew they'd never make the video shoot on time if they kept this up, so she playfully slapped at his hands. She was so glad Kaine felt the same way she did about him. But before she could convey, she'd been teasing him.

"Don't let Luka spoil what we have."

"Why would you say that?"

"It doesn't take a genius to see Luka cares for you. He's probably infuriated with me for bringing you back here and turned our evening into a romance and a headline. I don't blame him, though. But please remember to give me a chance before you believe whatever he says to you about me." Kaine warned, with the plea firm in his eyes. He stared at her in the mirror. His eyes were a stormy blue and serious considering their recent commitment.

Holly hadn't meant to seem reserved or removed from him. Then, she had rejected his offer — only because she wasn't up for torturing herself with a naked Kaine in the shower. Apparently, he'd realized she'd been playing, and teasing. But he hadn't liked it. She was sorry to cause him to doubt himself. And her silence made Kaine more uncomfortable because he cautioned her again.

"Remember, My Lady. Luka led you to believe women lined up to have sex with me when I wasn't. He doesn't always tell the truth."

"Kaine, I didn't want to bring this up, but you have to remember, Luka was sweet and kind to me when I first arrived. I don't want to do anything to lose his friendship."

"My Lady, we'll do the shoot as planned. So, forget him, and let me kiss you. Allow me remind you how I feel about my new girlfriend."

Holly shied away. "Kaine, it's difficult to resist you. I don't have much time to dress." She clarified, not truly understanding how, or why, everything seemed to move so fast.

"Naked is the way I prefer you," he retorted as he pulled the robe from her body dropping it to the floor. He had slipped his hands around her body seconds before he dropped a trail of warm kisses down her neck.

"Ummm, I love the way your neck tastes."

She watched him in the mirror.

He examined her reflection and directed his lust filled eyes to rake over her body. "I'm caught in a heat storm, My Lady," he admitted as he pulled away.

Holly could take no more of his ardent attention. She broke away from him, scooped up the robe, and headed for the bedroom, hoping she could stay away from him. He was casting his magical spell. He knew precisely what to say to her. And in her heart, she'd hated the thought of leaving him, even for the quick shower. As she crossed the carpet, she and agreed, "You're right, this attraction is creating a heat storm. Please, stay put, I have to get dressed, and I can't think straight when you're so close."

"Sure, My Lady, anything you wish. I promise." He stopped and threw her a naughty grin.

Inside the closet, she pulled on a pair of his 501 Levi's. They were long and baggy, and she rolled up the cuffs and cinched the belt tightly around her waist.

Not so sexy.

She slipped on a scarlet silk shirt with a banded collar over her bra. Holly checked herself in the mirror. Her breasts tingled and her nipples were unbearably sensitive after Kaine had awakened them with his delicious touch. They hardened again thinking about how she wanted to make him forget his promise not to ravish her this instant, but mostly to make her forget Luka.

No, she hadn't forgotten Luka. How could she ever forget? Her beautiful golden angel. She had to put Luka out of her mind. How else would she convince Kaine today she saw him, Kaine, the man? Or that she absolutely adored him?

Holly rescued a black silk vest of Kaine's tossed on the floor and slipped it on over the shirt. She walked out to sit on the edge of the bed and slipped into her damp heels.

She looked up to find Kaine standing in the doorway — watching her.

Chapter Twelve

LITTLE ANGEL

olly Hill became "Kaine Walker — Rock Star" official girlfriend. Outside the exclusive Lainesbough Hotel, print and film press swarmed as the vultures they were, hungry for fresh carrion — in this case, a glimpse of Kaine with his new girlfriend.

"Come here," Kaine called to her. "See them down there? They are ceremoniously gathering hoping to take a photograph, or record an interview with you, my mystery woman. Management must be delighted. They have spent millions making sure that no one in the entertainment world generates more press than I do. And since I finally have a woman in my life, the press will rage outside demanding that I name you."

Kaine's eyes narrowed and his tone of voice became cautious. "Speak to no one because the damned newshounds are ruthless. None of them can be trusted. You can count on them twisting your innocent words given any chance."

Holly understood the bitterness in his voice was from many years of hurtful misquotes by the tabloids, filled with half-truths and lies about him. Was this the time to tell him she had been surrounded by the media all of her professional life? How many lives had she seen ruined during a criminal trial after the media latched on with the tenacity of a pack of rabid dogs until the victim's reputation and money evaporated?

Kaine placed a comforting arm around her, pointed outside and explained, "As we speak, with no information to go on, networks are on overload trying to find out the basic statistics on you. This is one of the many reasons you'll come to learn why I'm so sorry you met me. From this point on, your life will never be the same. It will not be your own because the world believes it holds an exclusive right to have every detail about you."

No, this wasn't the time to tell him why she agreed that his words were correct. Or, that she brought more problems than he realized. Soon the media would learn who had won this contest. Holly Hill, from the infamous Collins' murder trial, and they would dig up her soon to be broken engagement to Brett Templeton. She read the headlines of the media's copy. It was becoming crucial that she speak with Brett. Blindsided was no way for him to learn she was no longer committed to their engagement.

Holly considered the situation, and she saw Kaine with worry simmering in his eyes because he was sorry to have dragged her into the baking limelight of the press. However, that was not her immediate concern. She pondered how sensational the Collins' murder trial had been in Europe. It was only a matter of time before she would find out.

Kaine's usually sweet, blue eyes sadden even more. "I'm so sorry they've found out about you so soon." He expressed his regret as he rested his chin on her head.

Should she make him understand? How she'd been thrown to the newspaper wolves during the Collins trial. A pinch of guilt assailed her, knowing she'd omitted a significant fact that her father was a newspaperman, a respected editor. Kaine was correct about one thing. The papers were working overtime to find out whom she was. She also understood Kaine's venom was mostly targeting the rags — the tabloid newspapers and entertainment TV shows. They had no ethical obligations or conscience when it came to exposing sensational stories, printing anything they could — forget the truth! Holly pulled away and stared into Kaine's worn and tired eyes that said they'd lost the battle, the press would win.

Kaine's passivity angered her.

Unexpectedly empowered, she decided to lay out her argument. "Kaine it doesn't matter to me what has happened to you in the past, and I haven't any idea what our future holds. All we have is now, and I'm happier than I've ever been in my life. Why — because I've met you, not in spite of that. You have brought a measure of happiness in a few hours I haven't enjoyed in a lifetime. I don't care about the press or your lifestyle. I'm here because I want to be with you. Therefore, I don't ever want to hear you say you're sorry I met you. Ever...."

The passion of her speech carried her away and fanned the flames of embarrassment, which quickly rose to flush her cheeks. She turned to move away and cautiously glanced up at Kaine.

Kaine quickly wrapped her in his arms and held her tightly in place, his eyes searching hers as if he couldn't believe her powerful words.

As if compelled, she added, "I do not lie My Lord — and, I couldn't lie to you." She dropped her head from his view.

His embrace nearly squeezed her life's breath from her

body.

"My Lady, those are words to fight for, and I have a strong intuition that the press will bloody well love you." He pulled her back and peered longingly into her eyes. "It won't be long, My Lady. I can see it in your eyes ... you can see me. Kaine, the man, because you've never known the other, a man in the press, the performer, or a man with a decadent past, and I dare to make another promise, it won't be long."

Holly understood what he meant. Kaine trusted her as well, at last. He trusted that she cared for him, not his many trappings that were holding him, hostage, keeping him as alone as Rapunzel trapped high in the tower.

She relaxed, leaning against him. "I'll go easy on the press."

Kaine laughed and declared, "Heaven help them ... from My Lady."

Holly glanced outside to the mounting troop that threatened to break through the security barriers set up to keep the fans at a safe distance from Kaine. This siege was like the hordes of media, and onlookers that swarmed outside the courthouse after each court session during the Collins' murder trial. The big difference, this time, they hunted her. The truth of the matter, the intimidation hit her hard, causing her to consider what had she gotten herself into this time. However, there wasn't any turning back. She'd made a decision, and that was Kaine.

No longer hidden on the top floor of the Lainesbough Hotel, burrowed in like outlaws, the suite phone rang for what seemed like the hundredth time. Holly understood this was a media war, held against their wills, as prisoners by the press. This isolation was a direct experience of what it was like to be a rock star or was this because he was Kaine. She realized that fame was not reported the way it truly was at all.

Kaine agreed with the caller. "Okay, down the back stairs to the ground floor. Yeah, we'll find it."

Kaine hung up and turned to Holly standing in the bedroom doorway, weaving the last of her long locks into a French braid. He suggested. "If you are ready for our second date, we will need to duck out the back. I'm not up to a barrage of questions, and it might be beneficial to let the press stew about you for a few hours."

"How do we get to the location?" Holly asked.

"It means we're slipping out the back. There won't be too many vultures waiting there," he stated and added, "if we're careful I don't think they'll even recognize us."

Holly followed Kaine around the suite preparing as outlaws for their escape. She helped him collect the last of his gear. He shoved all into his soft, Italian black leather satchel with a small Hurrikaine logo embossed in the corner.

He smiled a sexy grin as he slipped on his black leather motorcycle jacket. He threw her his leather letterman's Hurrikaine band jacket. "To keep you warm until I can."

Holly caught it midair and slid her arms deep into the oversized sleeves, drinking in his electrifying scent. An internal alarm was set off telling Holly to get out of the suite before she thought of ways to entice him to fulfill his promise sooner.

Kaine threw her a pair of Ray Ban sunglasses and grabbing his as they wrapped black scarves around their necks, and hurriedly took long strides down the hallway. His hand went out to hold her bent elbow, guiding her not to the end of the corridor to the elevator, but to take the stairway instead, to the ground floor. They headed out the rear of the hotel. A small van waited by the back door. It was open, exposing his Black Vincent motorcycle from the Hard Rock shoot.

"What do you think?" he asked.

She could almost see his chest swelling with pride. "Fabulous, let's go!" She cheered, and shot him an expectant smile.

"Great," he exclaimed, "a lady that likes leather, motorcycles, and lace."

It was not a description of her, she would have used three days ago, but this was the new, transformed Holly.

They climbed into the back of the van and exited the hotel under siege by the media. True to his word, they drove undetected past the crowd of press, and fans amassing out front. A few blocks away, the van stopped. A ramp shot out and dropped to the ground. Holly and Kaine screeched out of the van on his motorcycle and left the posse to eat their dust. They headed out of the city en route to the beautiful and enchanted English countryside, unnoticed.

Kaine's shiny black and chrome machine was a masterpiece. It was as powerful as he was and hummed comfortably beneath her. The cool, crisp, country air refreshed her spirit and caressed her flushed cheeks. Strands of her hair blew freely in the wind, and she held onto Kaine by squeezing her knees against his thighs.

After a while, she leaned forward to rest her head on his back. She tucked her hands inside his warm jacket pockets. How delightful it was to hold such a dear man while enjoying knoll after knoll of lush green fields and valleys, peppered with small farms and manors. Happy tears escaped from the corner of her eyes. She felt thankful for the precious time she'd be this close to him as the motorcycle carried her farther, and farther from anything, she'd ever known, deeper into the eye of the Hurrikaine.

TO BE CONTINUED...

Dear Reader,
Excited to read *DEVOTION (Part 3)?*
Please take a moment and leave a few comments about your favorite scenes wherever you purchased *TEMPTATION.* It is critical to the series to have feedback while the pleasure from the story is fresh in your mind. Thank you for your valuable support.
YOU ROCK!

A contented woman…

Holly Hill did not expect to become a girlfriend overnight, and spend a romantic night at magical Briarwood Castle.

A determined man…

Battle lines are drawn as Luka Hunter, a rock music executive enters into a rivalry with Kaine Walker for Holly's affections.

A dream man…

Kaine Walker, lead singer for the rock band Hurrikaine, has looked into thousands of eyes but found his future in Holly's.

What will Holly do when the dream man confesses?

Are his sweet words lies?

Find out in PROMISES (Part 3) London

http://www.kewtownsend.com/

KEW TOWNSEND

Affairs of the Heart Series ~ London

HEART (Part 1), *TEMPTATION* (Part 2)

Forthcoming:
PROMISES (Part 3), *DEVOTED* (Part 4), *BETRAYAL* (Part 5)

Ms. Townsend is a widow with a wonderful daughter, educator of school-age students, travel and movie buff, and writes romantic music fiction set in the 1960s-1980s rock scene in the *Affairs of the Heart Series*. She lives in sunny Southern California, where she loves to write under a palm tree with the wave's crashing along the shoreline.

KEW's love of rock music began at a very young age when she returned glass Coke bottles for change to buy 45 rpm records. Her interested moved from the music to the musicians. Living in Hollywood, she began her journey by interviewed the Beatles when they originally landed at Los Angeles International Airport. Acquiring a taste for the funny Englishmen, she eventually dated one of the Rolling Stones that exposed her to sex, drugs, and rock and roll. Later, her rock star memories surfaced in the *Affairs of the Heart Series* where she weaves her behind the scenes anecdotes with her long love of castles, mysteries, lightning, and thunder into a romantic suspense story. Her master's degree in Cultural Anthropology and Archaeology adds to her world travels, and flavor to her novels.

CONTACT KEW

kewtownsend.com

Leave a message, a review, and sign up for the NEWSLETTER. Be first to hear about new releases, preorders, sales, prizes, giveaways, and fun events.

www.ingramcontent.com/pod-product-compliance
Lightning Source LLC
Chambersburg PA
CBHW030635130626
46552CB00002B/860